Selected Stories

BOOKS BY N. V. M. GONZALEZ

The Winds of April

*Seven Hills Away**

*Children of the Ash-Covered
Loam and Other Stories*

A Season of Grace

*The Bamboo Dancers**

Look, Stranger, on This Island Now

*Selected Stories**

*Published in the United States by Alan Swallow

SELECTED
STORIES

N. V. M. GONZALEZ

Introduction by Leonard Casper

ALAN SWALLOW
DENVER

CONTENTS

ACKNOWLEDGMENTS

The first four of these stories appeared in the volume *Children of the Ash-Covered Loam,* Manila, The Benipayo Press, 1954; and the last three in the volume *Look, Stranger, on This Island Now,* Manila, Benipayo Press, 1963. All stories have had previous periodical publication as follows:

"Children of the Ash-Covered Loam" in *The Pacific Spectator* and *This Week Magazine* of the Manila *Chronicle.*

"The Morning Star" in *Stanford Stories 1950,* in *Life and Letters* (England), and in *This Week Magazine* of the Manila *Chronicle.*

"A Warm Hand" in *The Sewanee Review.*

"The Sea Beyond" in Manila *Sunday Times Magazine.*

"Come and Go," "The Bread of Salt," and "The Wireless Tower" appeared in *Philippines Free Press, Sunday Times Magazine* of Manila and the Manila *Chronicle This Week Magazine;* "The Bread of Salt" also appeared in *Meanjin* (Australia).

INTRODUCTION

LEONARD CASPER

In "The Bread of Salt" the boy-violinist feels deprived of all pride when his wealthy girl friend overcharitably forces fancy cakes on him, after he has played at her party. He returns to the street; to *pan de sal* — everyman's crisp, warm daily bread; and to the truth of himself. The same choice has been made so often by N. V. M. Gonzalez that it becomes his signature: to write of the simplest Filipino and what grace sustains him.

The stories in his first collection, *Seven Hills Away* (1947), seem by their near-static quality to suggest the slowness of change in the remotest burnt-over clearings, on islands just south of Manila but an epoch away. The deliberate sense of incompleteness in several of these tales represents, in part, peasant desperation; but also its compensations. For Gonzalez has written about the loneliness of the frontiersman as a traditional ritual in self-discovery and possession. A recurring theme in *Seven Hills Away* reveals that every departure is a return; every change, repetition. Each man finds his true self by fulfilling ancestral

5

patterns, as must his son too, some day, in lonely self-reliance. Part of the static quality of the stories, therefore, lies in the stoic nature of the characters, reassured by the realization that (as the history of national unity in the Philippines so well illustrates) each man is an island in an archipelago of human striving.

The folk quality of a people is so easily sentimentalized that Gonzalez has consistently felt required to place that quality under the most formal of restraints. Only once has such underwriting been used as a mode for characterizing someone other than the humblest of creatures. His satiric novel, *The Bamboo Dancers* (1959), chooses the flattest of styles to betray to the reader the inconsequentiality of its narrator, a modern *ilustrado* turned Fisher King in a post-Hiroshiman wasteland. Otherwise, Gonzalez' underwriting has always provided the primitive sense of experience, the very grain of a man in the act of growth.

He has never romanticized the hardness of life on overworked land or equatorial areas. It is a matter of record that the combination of abundant land and fertile waters, with the most outmoded methods of farming and fishing, is one source of Philippine poverty. Indeed the *kainginero* adds to his own misfortunes by burning over forested lands and thus inviting destruction by typhoon and flood. Nevertheless, without falsification, Gonzalez discovers consolations that humanize. In his first novel, *The Winds of April* (1941), it is a child's dream quietly adapting to an enlarging world that safeguards him, as his family moves along the island frontiers. His second novel, *A Season of Grace* (1956), commemorates the unconscious liaison that can grow between hardworking man and nature in its "eternal return." In one cycle of the seasons, the pioneer family prevails over a plague of rats and of human exploitations, because of a modesty and gentleness reminiscent of those pre-Spanish inhabitants of the Philippines whose social codes of justice and decency made possible their relatively easy conversion to Christianity. Even Gonzalez' language rhythms are those of untranslated speech, indebted in tempo, pause and prolonging to natural work rhythms, so that the candences themselves become indices of grace.

This same sense of quiet triumph distinguishes most of the stories in the present selection made from *Children of the Ash-Covered Loam* (1954) and *Look, Stranger, On This Island Now* (1963). Typically, his central characters are not the village elders, not the muscled champions, not the holders of vast estates; but the most vulnerable of the least — women and children — whose capacity for caring and whose outcries of hope mitigate the suffering of men. With the gradual increase of wisdom not unlike the oncoming of another season or the slow freshening of a woman's body, the young protagonist in "Children of the Ash-Covered Loam" encounters the source of life, the sacred mystery of reproduction. He finds it with equal amazement in his mother, the new rice in a *kaingin,* a littering sow. Marta, in "The Morning Star," bears her illegimate child — and the loss of that child — in a wilderness, her loneliness comforted by strangers and by her knowledge that birth and death are part of one turning wheel. She does not mock the American father who gave her, besides the child, only three woolen blankets. He was far from home; so is she now; so are the two sailors: each becomes the other's makeshift family. Hers is the homing instinct of Felipe who as a boy ran off to join the navy. Hers is the knowledge of one's ultimate aloneness, which Felipe only gradually learns through the insufficiency of his return and farewell and which the young, pregnant wife in "The Sea Beyond" violently accepts, as her husband dies beyond her reach and she and her longsuffering are impaled by the ruthless lights of a dockside jeep.

Marta apparently has achieved what all others yearn for, the fullness of identification: what the servant Elay, in "A Warm Hand," reaches for in the dark night; what prompts the boy Roberto, in "The Wireless Tower," to leave behind his valiant message — "To Whom It May Concern: I'll be up there."

N. V. M. Gonzalez has been the recipient of all major awards that the Philippines can bestow: the Commonwealth Literary Award (1941), the Republic Award of Merit (1954), the Republic Cultural Heritage Award (1960), and the Rizal Pro Patria Award (1961). Over the past twenty years he has been provided several Rockefeller grants, in order to travel, observe, and lecture in the United States and the Far East. He has been spending the current year in Rome, writing his fourth novel, on still another Rockefeller grant. If his work has received international recognition from Indonesia to Mexico, from the United States to Germany, the cause lies in Gonzalez's willingness to climb the tower alone, to see if lightning has struck; and to be able to say: It is true.

LEONARD CASPER

Boston College
Chestnut Hill, Mass.

CHILDREN OF THE ASH-COVERED
LOAM

ONE day when Tarang was seven, his father came home from Malig with the carabao Bokal, which belonged to their neighbor Longinos, who lived in the clearing across the river. The carabao pulled a sled which had a lone basket for its load.

"Harao!" his father said, pulling Bokal to a stop.

11

As Tarang ran to catch the lead rope that his father had tossed over to him, Bokal flared its nostrils and gave him a good look with its big watery eyes, as if to say, "Well, *Anak,* here we are! Have you been good?"

He had been playing alone in the yard, in the long slack of afternoon, and had been good, except that once Nanay had said why didn't he go up to the hut and do his playing there so that at the same time he could look after his little sister Cris, just now learning to crawl. But that was because Nanay had wanted to go there in the shade and pound rice, when what she ought to have done was wait for Tatay to help her, or wait for him to grow up, even! So what he had done was keep silence when she called. And then afterward she was spanking Cris for not taking an afternoon nap; and Tarang heard her calling to him: "You'll see when your *tatay* comes!" And so he walked to the riverbank and gathered some guavas, and ate the ripe ones as fast as he got them; and now he was belching, his breath smelling of guava. Perhaps his hair, too, smelled of guava, for why should Bokal flare its nostrils that way?

With Cris astride her hip, Nanay came down the hut, saying, "You might give that hard-headed son of yours a thrashing for staying out in the sunshine all afternoon."

But Tatay only laughed. "Really?" he said, and then asked, "That you would know what I've brought here!"

"What this time?" Nanay asked.

Tarang looked at the basket on the sled.

"If you must know, it's a pig!" Tatay said. He had unhitched the sled and was leading the carabao away to the *hinagdong* tree.

"Now don't you try touching it yet," his mother warned Tarang.

"It's so the boy will have something to look after," Tatay was saying from under the tree across the yard, where he had tethered the carabao.

From down the sled Tarang pulled the basket, and, indeed, two black feet presently thrust out of it. The corner of the basket had a big hole, and now there sprang forth another foot.

Tatay cut the basket open with his bolo, and the pig struggled out. "It's for you to look after," he told the boy.

Nanay was standing there beside him and, having swung Cris over to her other hip, began scratching the belly of the pig with her big toe.

"Do this quite often, and it will become tame," she said. And to Tatay: "Now if you hold Cris awhile—"

Then she took the bolo and, crossing the yard, she went past the hinagdong tree where Bokal was and into the underbrush. She returned with six freshly ripe papayas; she wanted then and there to cut them up and feed the pig with them. But Tatay said, "Here, you hold Cris yourself."

He got back his bolo from Nanay, slipped it into its sheath, and hurried down the path to the *kaingin*. Tarang could see the tall dead trees of the clearing beyond the hinagdong tree and the second growth. The afternoon sun made the bark of the trees glisten like the bolo blade itself.

He thought his father would be away very long, but Tatay was back soon with a length of tree trunk which had not been completely burned that day they set fire to the clearing. The fire had devoured only the hollow of the trunk, so that what Tatay had brought really was a trough that the kaingin had made. Now Tatay cut the ends neatly and flattened one side so that the trough would sit firm on the ground.

They all sat there watching the pig eating off the trough. In a short while its snout was black from rubbing against the burned bottom and sides.

"Where did this pig come from? You have not said one word," Nanay said.

"Well, there I was in the barrio. And whom do I see but Paula — when all the time I meant not to get even a shadow of her."

Tarang stared at both of them, not knowing what they were talking about. Cris sat on Nanay's arm, watching the pig also, and making little bubbling sounds with her mouth.

"We shall pay everything we owe them next harvest," Nanay said.

"Well, there I was and she saw me," Tatay went on. "She asked could I go to her house and have my noon meal there? So I went, and ate in the kitchen. Then she asked could I fetch some water and fill the jars? And could I split some firewood? And could I go out there in the corner of her yard and have a look at her pigs?

"She had three of them, one a boar," Tatay went on. "And if I wasn't afraid really that I'd be told to fix the fence or the pen, I am a liar this very minute."

"But for a ganta or five chupas of salt, maybe. Why not?" Nanay asked.

"You guess right. She said, 'Fix it, for the ganta of salt that you got from the store last time.' "

"Well, there you are!"

"That's the trouble, there I was. But she said: 'For your little boy to look after — if you like. Yes, why not take one sow with you?' And I said: 'For my boy?' Because, believe me, I was proud and happy Paula remembered my anak. She said: 'If you can fatten it, let it have a litter; then all the better for us.' So I've brought home the pig."

Nanay threw more bits of ripe papaya into the trough. Tarang scratched the pig's back gently as it continued to eat, making loud noises, not only with its mouth but also with something else inside its belly.

"If there is a litter, we are to have half," his father was saying; and then his mother said:

"That is good enough."

"Well, then, feed it well, Anak!" his father said.

"And you said, there was a boar in that pen?" his mother asked.

"A big and vigorous boar," his father said.

Nanay smiled and then walked over to the kitchen to start a fire in the stove. When the pig had devoured all the ripe papayas, Tatay got a rope and made a harness of it round the pig's shoulder.

"Here, better get it used to you," Tatay said.

So Tarang pulled the rope and dragged the pig across the yard. His father led the way through the bush, to the edge of the kaingin nearest the hut. There they tied the pig to a tree stump. Then his father cut some stakes to make the pen with.

They did not make a full-fledged pen, only one with two sides, because, for the other two sides, they used the outcropping roots of an old *dao* tree. The rest was easy; it was Tarang who shoved the pig inside when the pen was ready. Afterward his father went back to the hut to get the trough..

He fed the pig with ripe papayas as well as green, and the good thing was that Tatay did not become cross with him whenever the bolo had to be used. He would strap it round his waist and go out there in the bush himself. Sometimes he brought home *ubod* from the betel nut or the sugar palm, and the soft parts of the ubod Nanay usually saved up for supper while the hard parts she allowed him to take to the pig. There was the rice husk, too. Before, it did not matter whether or not, after pounding the rice, Nanay saved the chaff; from the mortar she would take the rice in her wide, flat winnowing basket and, with the wind helping her, clean the grains right there under the hinagdong tree at the edge of the yard. But from now on it would not do to leave the rice husk there on the ground. The kitchen wash mixed with rice husk was a favorite of the sow's; and for ever so long after feedingtime, you could see her wear, a brown band of rice husk round her mouth.

One day Nanay came home from the kaingin with welts across her cheek and over the valley of her nose. Had someone struck her with a whip? Tatay did not seem worried. He laughed at her, in fact, and Nanay had to say something.

"I only went to the thicket for some rattan with which to fix the pen."

"Now which pen?" Tatay asked.

"The sow's."

Tatay said, "You could have waited for us; that was work for us."

"Still, work that had to be done," Nanay

said. "And but for the swelling of the sow's belly, what do you think could have happened?"

"We had thought of the swelling of the belly," Tatay said.

"Still, I had to get the rattan," Nanay said.

"And hurt your face," Tatay said, touching gently the scratches on the skin.

Tarang also touched the valley of her nose. She continued: "I stepped on a twig. Then a vine sprang from nowhere and struck me."

Tatay laughed over that one heartily. "It was as though you had stolen something, and then somebody had gone after you and caught you!"

"Next time, I leave the pen alone," Nanay said.

But during the days that followed they were all too busy with work in the kaingins to bother with anything else, really. In the near-by kaingins, people had started planting; and so that they would come over to help later on, Tatay and Nanay were often away out there working. That left Tarang alone in the hut, alone to cook his own meals and fetch water from the well near the riverbank; although it was hardly midafternoon, he would start for the underbrush in search of ubod or ripe papayas. Before the sun had dropped behind the forest, he had fed his sow.

He was walking down the path from the kaingin one afternoon when he saw Tia Orang in the hut. He had seen her many times before, on days when Nanay and Tatay took him to the barrio, and he was not a little frightened of her then. The old midwife wore a hempen skirt dyed the color of tan bark, which is like brown clay; and so were her blouse and kerchief.

"And where would they be?" she asked the boy.

"Across the river."

"Where exactly? I have come for the planting."

"In the clearing of Mang Longinos, perhaps," the boy said. "We are not yet planting."

"Now be good enough to give me a drink

of water, Anak," the old midwife said. "Then I shall be on my way."

She reached for the dipper of water that he brought her. She drank, and then, putting down the dipper, tweaked Tarang on the leg. "If I do not see your mother, Anak, tell her that Tia Orang has come. Tell of my passing through, and of my helping in the planting when the time comes."

For a long time afterward Tarang remembered how they spent morning after morning in the kaingin, gathering pieces of burned wood and piling them up and then burning them again. Some pieces were too heavy to lift, even with all three of them — Nanay, Tatay, and himself — helping together; other pieces were light enough, and he would take them to the edge of the clearing, where his father laid out a fence by piling the wood between freshly cut staves and keeping these in place with rattan.

It was a pity to have Cris left behind in the hut, tied to the middle of the floor, lest she should crawl over to the steps, down the dirt of the kitchen, past the stove box, then over to the threshold, and finally out to the yard; often they returned to the hut to find her asleep, some portion of string wound tight round her legs.

But, one morning, instead of leaving Cris behind, Nanay took her to the kaingin. That was the day Tatay left the hut very early and returned after breakfast with a white pullet under his arm, and then he and Nanay had a quarrel.

"You have found the chicken in the river bed? Is that what you might say?" she demanded.

"I came from Longinos' place, if you must know."

"And that pullet?"

"Look into your hamper," Tatay said.

Nanay pulled out the hamper from the corner and, in the half-light from the window, opened it and looked through her clothes one by one.

"The *camisa* that Paula gave me, it's gone," she said, almost in tears.

"A camisa seven years too worn out, what matter now?" Tatay laughed at her.

"So you bartered it for a pullet — for that *dumalaga?*" Nanay said.

"It will bring luck, have no regrets," Tatay said.

They followed him to the kaingin, but when they reached the edge, where the fence was waist-high, Tatay asked Tarang's mother to stay behind. They left Cris and her sitting on a log at the edge of the fence. Tarang followed Tatay past the dao tree where the pigpen was, and the smell of the trough followed him to the middle of the kaingin.

Tatay stopped near a tree stump that was knee-high and motioned to him to get no closer, for now he was holding the dumalaga with one hand, letting its wings flap like pieces of rag in the clearing breeze, and he had pulled out his bolo. No, Tarang couldn't get any closer. Tatay laid the pullet's neck upon the flat of the tree stump and without a word cut the head off. Was that a red streak that cut an arc toward the ash-covered ground? Tatay held the headless pullet higher, to let the blood spurt out a long way.

"Go, Evil Spirits of the land! Go, now!" Tatay was saying. "Now this land is ours! We shall make it yield rich crops!"

Tarang looked back in the direction where Nanay and Cris sat waiting, and at first he did not see them. Beyond the clearing's edge loomed the half-dark of the forest, and a cloud had covered the rising sun and changed the morning to early evening.

Tatay had put back his bolo into its sheath and was calling for Nanay and Cris to come.

"Then we start planting now?" Nanay asked.

"You three wait here, for I myself am strong enough for the getting of the seed," Tatay said, and walked down the trail to the hut.

He returned with Tio Longinos and Tia Pulin and Tia Adang, and they were all of them provided with short wooden sticks sharpened at the ends for making holes in the ground. Tarang made one of his own, but he was not good at using it. He was as slow as Nanay, who could hardly bend from having to have Cris astride her hip. After a while his stick got blunted, and Tatay said he should sharpen it again. Tatay handed him the bolo. But when Tarang started to sharpen the stick, his hand began to tremble. Cold sweat gathered on his brow, and the ash-covered ground seemed raw with the smell of the chicken's blood.

"You and Cris," Tatay said, taking the bolo from him, "you stay in the shade and let your mother work."

And so they looked for the shadiest buri palm at the edge of the kaingin. Nanay cut some dry leaves and set them on the ground, and there she set Cris also, and said to Tarang, "Keep your sister from crying, at least."

But, of course, he could do nothing to stop her, and Cris cried herself hoarse. She would not let him hold her; they chased each other round and round, even beyond the boundary of the leaves. It hurt his knees crawling. What stopped her finally was the sound that the wind made as it passed through and over the palm leaves; for it was a strange sound, like that of drums far away.

Toward noon Tatay called everyone together. They gathered in the hot sun near the tree stump where the dumalaga had been killed. Already Tio Longinos and Tia Pulin and Tia Adang were gathered there when Nanay, who had gone to pick up Cris, reached the tree stump.

"Keep out of the way, Anak," Tatay said, for Longinos was setting up a small cross made of *banban* reeds.

He stepped back, but not so far away as not to hear; Longinos was now talking to the cross.

"Let citronella grass give fragrance," he was saying, pulling a sheaf of the grass from the pouch at his waist, where he kept his betel nut and chewing things. Likewise, he took from the pouch other things. "Let ginger appease the Evil Ones. Let iron give weight to the heads of rice on this clearing."

Tarang edged closer, using his father's arm, which was akimbo, as a window to peep from.

And he saw the bits of ginger and the three pieces of nails that Longinos had placed at the foot of the reed cross.

"Too hot it is now to work, isn't it?" Longinos said, grinning away his tiredness. His face glistened with sweat, and he led the way, making a new path across the ash-covered ground.

Tarang brought up the rear, and he saw many holes that the sticks had made which had not been properly covered. He stopped and tapped the seed grains gently in with his big toe. He wandered about in this way; eyes to the ground, quick to catch the yellow husk of the grains. They were like bits of gold against the gray of the ashy ground. He would stop and press each little mound of grain gently, now with his left big toe, now with his right. Shorter and shorter his shadow grew until it was no more than a blot on the ground, moving as deftly as he moved among the tree stumps and over the burned-out logs.

He heard much talking back and forth afterward about how Tatay had planted the clearing a little too soon, that Tia Orang ought to have come. That they might have waited for her, Nanay said. But what was done was done, Tatay argued.

That afternoon they visited the kaingin. After he had brought the feed for his sow, Tarang followed Nanay and Tatay; it seemed to him that the ground was so dry it could well be that he was walking on sand. Nanay said that ants would soon make off with the grain.

That evening they sat outside, in the yard. They watched the sky. There were no stars. Black night covered the world; somewhere to the west, beyond the mountain range, rain had come. Twice lightning tore at the darkness, as though a torch were being used to burn some dry underbrush in a kaingin up there in the clouds.

They had an early supper because Nanay said that, if a storm should come, it would be difficult to do any cooking in the stove, now that its roof of buri leaves had been dried up and had become loose shreds these many

months of the hot season. They went to bed
early, too.

"There, what's done is done!" Tatay said,
and sat on the mat, cocking his ears.

It was the rain. Tarang thought he might
watch it, only it was rather late in the night.
He was tired and sleepy still.

Tatay, of course, had rushed to the window, hoping perhaps to see the rain shoot ar-
rows across the yard.

Now, Tarang could hardly keep himself
from getting up also. He got as far as the window when his mother awoke and called him
sternly back to bed. He had to content him
self listening to the rain on the roof.

It proved a brief rain burst only. Before
daybreak it was all over.

"There is work for us to do, don't you
know?" Tatay said after breakfast, knotting
his bolo string round his waist. "The pig —
your sow, understand? With the rains now
coming—"

Tarang understood readily that they must
have a roof over the pen. He set out eagerly,

doing everything that his father bade him. Tatay gathered the buri leaves, and these had to
be taken one by one to the foot of the dao tree
where the pen was. So while Tatay disappeared in the bush to get some vines to use for
tying the leaves onto the makeshift beams, Tarang struggled with the leaves. He dragged
them through the bush one by one, making the
noise of a snake running through a *kogon* field.

They were not quite through with the roof
when the sky darkened again. From afar thun-
der rumbled; only the storm seemed rather close
this time.

It was a long dreary-looking afternoon. It
was warm, but he knew that soon it would be
raining very hard, perhaps as hard as he had
ever seen rain fall before. When Tarang set
out to gather ripe papayas for his sow, it was
already drizzling, and Nanay had to make him
promise not to stay long.

He came running to the house. The thunderstorm was right behind him. Panting, he
strode into the kitchen, unknotting the string of
his father's bolo from his waist.

"Mind to look for mushrooms tomorrow," Tatay was saying.

Why, do mushrooms come with thunderstorms? Tarang wondered. All through supper he asked about mushrooms, and now it seemed that with each flash of lightning the million and one mushrooms that grow wild the whole world over pushed their spongy little umbrellas an inch or so toward the sky.

The drizzle was heavier now, and an owl kept hooting somewhere beyond the bamboo brakes across the river. Then the calls stopped. Tarang and his father sat there before the stove box watching Nanay, who was starting to cook rice for supper. Already the real rain was here.

There was the sound of shuffling feet in the yard, and when Nanay looked through the open door, she said, "Why, it is Tia Orang!"

The old woman dropped the frond of buri that she had used for an umbrella in the rain and clambered up the hut. Nanay called out to Tatay, who had gone to the pigpen to see that the roof they had fixed over it was firm enough and would not be blown away should strong winds come along with the rain as they often did.

"The midwife is here," Nanay called. And to Tia Orang: "Now you must stay the night with us."

The other said, "Then, how goes life with you?"

"The same."

"Don't I see a change? Don't I see life growing with you?

Tarang sat there by the stove fire, idly tending the pot of vegetable stew for supper.

Nanay was saying, "There's nothing in me to be seen!" And, passing her hand up and down her belly: "Look, nothing at all! Nothing yet!"

"Cris is hardly two, that's why? But—" the old one became a little excited — "but time enough, time enough!"

"Then, let it be," Nanay said.

"And when it's time, I will surely remember to come," Tia Orang said.

Tatay appeared at the door carrying a buri

umbrella of his own. He greeted Tia Orang with much show of respect.

"To be sure," he said, "let her stay the night with us," he told Nanay. "Now, is supper ready?" He turned to Tarang, asking, "Anak, is the supper ready?"

So Nanay came down, leaving Cris upstairs with Tia Orang, and helped get the supper ready. She removed the pot of vegetable stew from the fire and started pouring some of it into the bowls. There were not enough bowls for all five of them, including Cris, and Nanay said Tarang should use the coconut-shell dipper for the drinking water.

"But," Tia Orang asked, laughing, "should not I first of all earn my supper, no?"

Nanay had almost everything ready — the rice, and then a little pinch of salt on a banana leaf, and the bowls of stew, all of these on the bamboo floor.

"If you want to," Nanay said; "do I spread the mat?"

"If you want to," Tia Orang said.

"It is bound to come, it is bound to come!"

Tia Orang said, kneeling on the mat, one hand pressing Nanay's abdomen. She beckoned to Tatay: "Be of help!"

It was as if Tatay had been waiting all this time. He was ready with a coconut shell containing the bits of crushed ginger roots soaked in oil. Tia Orang dipped her fingers into the mess, then rubbed her palms together, and commenced kneading the muscles of Nanay's belly. The smell of ginger root and coconut oil made Tarang sneeze. The shell with the medicine Tarang remembered from the many occasions Nanay appeared to be ill, and the kneading was just about as familiar. Tatay did exactly the same whenever any one of them had pains in the stomach.

Tatay had lighted the *lamparilla* and set it on the floor, upon an empty sardine can. In the light, which was yellow like the back part of a leaf just starting to become dry, Tia Orang's face looked as though made of earth.

Nanay was smiling at her. She lay smiling at everyone, her eyes traveling from one face to the next. A blush reddened her cheeks.

Tia Orang and Nanav talked, but mostly in whispers. Tarang caught only a few words. Then, aloud, the old woman called to Tatay, and Nanay got up and rolled up the mat. She let it rustle softly.

"Let us have supper now, no?" Tatay asked.

Wind from the open doorway fanned the wood in the stove, and, because this was bright enough, Tatay blew the lamparilla out.

They sat round the plate of rice that Nanay had set earlier on the floor. Tarang felt his hunger grow with each mouthful of rice, and he ate heartily, sipping the broth of the vegetable stew, then mixing the rice with the tomatoes and the sweet-potato leaves and the dried anchovies, gray and headless, in his coconut-shell bowl.

Tia Orang talked a great deal. Perhaps to conceal her appetite, Tarang thought. She talked about the old days in Malig, those days when people did not go so far inland as Loob-Loob but stayed most of the time in the barrio or else went only as far as Bakawan. Tarang

listened because she spoke of Evil Ones and of
Spirits, and he remembered the kaingin and
Longinos and the citronella and the nails and
ginger root.

"Now there was that man once lost his
arm felling a tree," Tia Orang was saying, "and
another, forgetting his reed cross and all those
things of the *gapi,* who began to suffer a strange
sickness."

Tarang cocked his ears.

"That he began to throw pus instead of
water, let me tell you. Do you know what happened, also, to his wife? Well, the woman was
with child. And when she was about to deliver, the misfortune came. No child came
forth, but when the labor was done, there were
leeches and nothing else! Fat and blood-red,
and they filled a whole wooden bowl."

Nanay stopped eating suddenly. She
reached out for drinking water, which was in
a coconut shell laid there also upon the floor.
Tatay ate in silence, leaving nothing in his bowl.
He looked up at Tia Orang as if to ask: "Now,
what else?"

Outside, it was as though someone with a brightly burning torch were driving bees off a hive up there in the sky. Beyond the western mountains was another early evening thunderstorm.

At the corner where Nanay was spreading a sleeping mat for Tia Orang, the wind brushed the siding of buri leaves. "Mind to gather those mushrooms tomorrow, just as I've said," Tatay kept telling her.

They went to bed very early. Tarang thought he should stay in one corner, far from Nanay. He was a man now, he felt.

He took an empty buri sack, the one for keeping palay in, and pressed it flat with his feet. It made a nice bed on the floor, there against the wall, near the doorstep.

On her mat Tia Orang stirred wakefully, but she could be heard snoring. Many times Tarang awoke, the strange noises in the old woman's nose and mouth frightening him not a little. It was as if she were uttering strange words to strangers, to people who did not belong to the world of men and women. Tarang strained his ears, but he could not catch even one word; yet there was no doubt that she was talking to someone even now in her sleep. She stirred and turned to the wall, and now she was talking to the buri leaves with which the wall was made.

The thunderstorm came closer. For the first time since he could remember, the rain poured with loud thuds on the roof. It must be falling all over the forest, too, he thought; all over the empty river and as far down as the swamps that surrounded the barrio of Malig by the sea.

In his mind, half-awake, Tarang thought the rain was making music now, shaking songs off the swaying treetops on the fringe of the kaingin. Then he heard Tatay get up from bed. Perhaps Tatay, too, had heard the music of the rain. Only Tatay was hurrying down the hut, knotting his bolo string round his waist as he slipped past the door.

Tarang thought he could hear something else besides — for instance, the sow in the pen, under the dao tree. He listened more carefully.

He could hear the grunting. There were little noises, too. A squirming litter, protesting against the cold. Surely, with wet snouts tugging at its teats, a sow could be annoyed. The belly would be soft like a rag.

"That's something to see!" He got up quietly and slipped out the door into the rain.

It seemed that at this very hour the rice grains, too, would be pressing forward, up the ash-covered loam, thrusting forth their tender stalks through the sodden dirt. He thought he caught the sound that the seeds also made.

The ground was not too wet. In his haste, Tarang struck a tree stump with his big toe; and the hurt was not half as keen as it might have been, not half as sharp as his hunger for knowing, for seeing with his own eyes how life emerged from this dark womb of the land at this time of night.

THE MORNING STAR

T HE sailor went back to the outriggered boat and returned with a lantern. It lighted up the footpath before him and his flat unshod feet. He walked in a slow, shuffling manner, the lantern in his hand swinging in rhythm.

"Can't you walk faster?" the old man shouted from the coconut grove.

Instead of saying something in reply, the sailor shuffled on, neither hastening nor slowing his gait.

41

"You're a turtle, that's what," said the old man.

As the sailor approached, the lantern light caught the entrance of the makeshift shelter. Then the oval of light completely engulfed the shelter, which was shaped like a pup tent and built of coconut leaves woven into loose shingles. A matting of coconut leaves was spread on the ground, and walking across it, the old man hung the lantern from a ridgepole at the far end. A woman sat in one corner, her back half-turned to the entrance.

"Now if you aren't stupid. Quite like a turtle, really," the old man said to the sailor.

"Ha?" the other said, with a twang.

The old man had expected that; there was something wrong with the sailor's tongue. "And how about the jute sacks and the blankets?" the old man said. "Didn't I tell you to get them?"

"Ha?" came the sailor's reply.

"Stop it!" said the old man, angrily. "If you weren't born that way, I'd give you a thrashing." He waved him away. "Be off! And while you are at it, bring over some water.

There's no saying whether we'll find drinking water hereabouts. Would you care for supper, Marta?"

"No, thank you," said the woman in the hut.

"It'll be best to get some food ready, though," said the old man. "We've salmon in the boat."

The sailor had shuffled away, the coconut fronds on the ground rustling softly as he stepped on them.

"Bring over a tin of salmon. And also the pot of rice we have on the stove box," the old man called after the sailor.

From somewhere a bird uttered a shrill cry; and the old man spoke to the woman again. "If you'll step out of there just a while, Marta...."

"I am quite comfortable here, Uncle," she said.

"But you should be walking about, instead of sitting down like that."

"It seems better here," said the woman. But later she said: "All right."

"I'll build a fire," the old man said.

The bird's call came again, in a note of wild urgency. "That's the witch bird. I can tell for certain," the woman said. "They take newborn children away."

"No, it's not the witch bird," the old man said.

He gathered some dry leaves and twigs and in a minute had a fire blazing.

"Still, it's a fine time for having a baby, Uncle. Isn't it?"

"It's God's will," the old man said. Marta was laughing at herself. "We'll do the best we can. Walk about, stretch your legs; hold on to a coconut trunk over there, if it hurts you so."

"I'm quite all right, Uncle," said Marta.

The fire crackled, and the old man added more leaves and twigs. The blaze illumined the large boles of the coconut palms.

The clear sky peered through the fronds of the palms but there were no stars. The night had a taut, timorous silence, disturbed only by the crackling of the fire.

The woman walked up and down, not venturing beyond the space lighted up by the fire. She was a squat, well-built woman. Her arms and legs were full-muscled, like those of a man. If she had cut her hair and worn trousers instead of a skirt, she would have passed for a man. Her distended belly and large breasts would not have made any difference.

The old man watched her with unending curiosity. Like him, she wore a field jacket, the sleeves rolled up, being too long. Her skirt was of a thick olive-drab material, made from fatigues that some American soldier had discarded.

"Is that his name printed on there?" the old man asked.

In the firelight the letters "Theodore C. Howard" could be read in white stencils on the back of the drab green jacket.

"Oh, no, Uncle," said Marta. "This isn't his. He gave me three woolen blankets, though."

"That's fair," said the old man.

"What do you mean, Uncle? Please don't tease me," said Marta.

"Well, others do get more than that. For their labor, I mean. You worked as a laundry woman?"

"Yes, Uncle," Marta replied. "But afterwards we lived together. Three weeks. We had a hut near Upper Mangyan. You could see the whole camp of the Army from there." With her hands, she held on to her belt, a rattan string, as she spoke. "It pains so, at times. Well, I washed clothes for a living, Uncle. That's what I went there for."

"Did you earn any money?"

"No, Uncle. I'm never for making money. He said one day, 'Here are twenty pesos,' " she said with a laugh. "He had a way of talking to me and never saying my name, as though I had no name. The others, the ones I only washed clothes for, had a nickname for me. 'Sweet Plum,' I remember. That's how they called me. 'Sweet Plum.' What's a 'plum,' Uncle? They say it's a fruit."

"I don't know," said the old man. "In our country, we have no such fruit."

"He would not call me 'Sweet Plum,' even. And, as I said, he wanted to give me the money. 'What for?' I said. And he said, 'For your mother.' But I have no mother, I told him so. 'Well, for your father and brothers and sisters.' But I have no such folk. I told him so. I said, 'Keep your money. I love you, so keep your money.' And he was angry, and he swore and then left the hut. I never saw him again, but he left me three woolen blankets."

The old man listened to the story with great interest, but now that it was over he made no comment, beyond getting up and thoughtfully tending the fire.

"No, Uncle. You're wrong to think I ever earned money," Marta said. She walked a few steps and returned to the fireside. "By the way, Uncle, how much does it cost to go to San Paulino in your boat?"

"That's where you live?"

She nodded.

"For you, nothing. Not a centavo."

"I can give you one of my woolen blankets."

"The trip will cost you nothing."

"Of course, you'll say, 'What a foolish woman she is! To think that she does not know when her time comes!' But truly, Uncle, the days are the same to me. The nights are the same. I can't count days and months. Maybe, Uncle, I'll never grow old. Do you think I'll ever grow old?"

The old man did not know what to say. A soft chuckle, and that was all.

"And I am going home. Am I not foolish, Uncle?"

To humor her, the old man said: "Yes, you are quite foolish. A good thing you found my boat, no?"

"I feel lucky, yes," Marta said. "I must leave, that was all. Maybe, it isn't my time yet. The long walk from Upper Mangyan, and then three days on the beach, before finding your boat.... Maybe, this is only the seventh month. How long is nine months, Uncle?"

The old man wished he could give a good answer. "Nine months," he said finally.

"I understand. You old men know a lot. Now, don't laugh, Uncle. I've been married before, and this man I married was an old man, too. May he rest in peace. Oh, it pains so! Here, right here!" She indicated the approximate location of the pain.

"Walking relieves it, so they say."

The leaves crackled softly on the ground as she trod upon them with her bare feet. She went back and forth, and talked on as if to amuse herself.

"Now, this man was a tailor. You see, I worked as a servant in a rich man's house. And this tailor said, one day, 'You don't have to work so hard like that, Marta. Come live with me.' Ah, you men are tricky. Aren't you, Uncle?"

"Sometimes," the old man couldn't help saying. "Some men are, I must say," he agreed readily.

"This tailor, he saw how industrious I was — and, I dare say, I am. Because God made me so; with the build of an animal, how can one be lazy? There's not a kind of work you men can do that I can't do also. That's a woman for you! My tailor was pleased with me. I was a woman and a man all in one, and he was so happy he stopped becoming a tailor and took instead to visiting with neighbors, talking politics and things like that." She stopped, and then as if suddenly remembering something: "But he left me no child. Oh, he fooled me so, Uncle!"

"Well, you'll have one soon, I must say," said the old man.

"As I was saying, I lived with this old tailor. He was a widower and had been lonely, and now he was kind to me. But he died of consumption — he had it for a long time — the year the war started. I went back to the rich man's house where I had worked before. When the Americans came back I said to this rich man, 'I am going away. Only for a short time, though. I hear they pay well at the camp of the Army, if you can wash clothes and do things like that. When I have enough money,

I'll come back.' That's what I said. Oh, oh! It hurts so!"

"It's time the sailor returns," said the old man. "Does it pain much?"

"Ah, but pain never bothers me, Uncle. Didn't I tell you I am built like an animal? This tailor, he used to beat me. I didn't care. I can stand anything, you know. I chopped wood and pounded rice for him. I was quite sorry when he died. That's the truth, Uncle."

She stopped and laughed, amused more than ever perhaps at the way she had been talking. The old man looked at her quizzically.

"And you'll bring this baby home to San Paulino?" he said.

"Why, of course, Uncle. It'll be so tiny, so helpless — you know. Why do you ask?"

The old man hesitated, but in the end he decided to tell her: "There are places — in the city, for example — where they'll take care of babies like that...."

"But can they take care of him better than I? That's impossible, Uncle," the woman said,

exictedly. "Oh, it hurts so! — I do like — oh!
— to look after him myself...."

The firelight caught her faint smile. She
had a common-looking face, but her eyes were
pretty and big and smiling.

She had stopped talking. The sailor appeared in their midst, saying, "Ha!"

"Warm the salmon in the fire," said the
old man.

He took the jute sacks and the blankets
into the shelter and prepared a bed. Outside,
in the light of the fire, the sailor opened the
salmon can with his bolo and began drinking
the soup in the can.

"Can't you wait for me?"

The old man crawled out of the hut, annoyed partly because the sailor had begun to
eat and partly because Marta was groaning.

"Don't wail there like a sow," he told her
gruffly.

Then he sat before the pot of rice that the
sailor brought over.

"A sow doesn't wail so, Uncle," said the
woman innocently.

The old man said nothing in reply. He and the sailor ate hurriedly, making noises with their mouths.

"Ha!" said the sailor, in that helpless way of his. looking in Marta's direction.

"She doesn't care for food. She said so," the old man explained. And to Marta, he said: "If it's too much to bear, you may go in. We'll keep some of the salmon for you. Afterwards you'll be so hungry."

Marta followed his advice, crawling into the hut. Her head struck the lantern that hung from the ridgepole, and for a while it swung about, the oval of light dancing on the ground.

"I'll be with you in a minute," said the old man. "Why you've to let me do this, I don't know." It seemed he had become a different person from the *uncle* Marta knew a while ago; he felt the change in himself.

"Uncle," the woman called from in the shelter, "what's a man called when he does a midwife's business?"

The old man was washing his mouth with water from the container the sailor had brought from their outriggered boat. When he was through, he said: "You horrible creature! I'm now sure of it! You've fooled me. You planned all this.... You're more clever than I thought...."

There was silence in the shelter. From afar the night bird called again, clearly and hauntingly. The sailor, calling the old man's attention to the bird, said, "Ha, ha!" He pointed with his finger at the darkness, but the old man did not mind him.

The silence grew tense, although there were soft noises from the shelter, noises that the movement of feet and arms and body made upon the matting, as if a sow were indeed lying there to deliver a litter. The lantern glow fell full upon the woman's upraised knees. She had covered them with a blanket.

"Uncle!" she called frantically.

Before going in the old man looked up at the sky. There was a lone star at last, up in the heavens. He could see it through the palm fronds. He'd like to remember that. He wished he could see a moon, too, and that he knew for

certain how high the tide was at the beach;
for, later, he'd recall all this. But there were
no other signs. There was only this star.

"I'm so frightened, Uncle," Marta was saying, her voice hoarse and trembling. "And it
hurts so! Uncle, it will be the death of me!"

"Stop this foolish talk," said the old man
angrily. "Pray to God. He is kind," he said.

His hands and knees were shaking. He
knelt beside Marta, ready to be of assistance.

"Oh — oh — oh! Uncle, I want to die,
I want to die!" she cried, clutching his hand.

When the sailor heard the squall of the
child he said "Ha, ha," with joy. He wanted
to see the child, but the old man told him to
go away.

"Go!" the old man said, waving his arms.

The sailor returned to his sleeping place
and lay as before. The night was warm and
restful, and soon he was fast asleep.

The old man joined him under the coconut tree, their feet touching and pointing toward
the smouldering fire. Through the palm fronds
the old man could see the sky growing light,

for soon it would be morning. The star peered at him as before, through the thick coconut palm leaves. It had watched over them all this time.

The old man turned and using his arm for a pillow tried to sleep. The sailor was snoring peacefully. The old man could see Marta in the shelter, her legs flat on the mat and the child in a bundle beside her.

The old man fell asleep thinking of the child, for it was a boy. A gust of wind woke him up, and when he opened his eyes he did not realize at first where he was. He felt glad he had been of help to the woman, and he wondered if in any way he had been unkind to her. He wished he had not called her a sow and had been gentle with her. He sat up and saw the lantern in the shelter.

"Are you all right?" he called, for he heard the woman stir.

She did not answer but sat up, moving in a slow, deliberate way, her shadow covering the child like a blanket.

"It's the witch bird, Uncle," she said in a tired, faraway voice. "Did you hear the witch bird? Now he is dead — Uncle, he is dead!"

The old man lowered the lantern. It had a faint blue flame. The baby beside her was limp and gray like the blanket wrapped around it.

"You're a sow, that's what you are! God Almighty," he crossed himself, "may You have mercy on us!"

"Believe me, Uncle.... It's the witch bird...."

The sailor had wakened. He got up and sat hugging his knees and stared at the old man.

"You build a fire, turtle!" the old man shouted at him. "Don't you see it's so dark?"

"Ha!" the sailor said.

A WARM HAND

HOLDING on to the rigging, Elay leaned over. The dinghy was being readied. The wind tore her hair into wiry strands that fell across her face, heightening her awareness of the dipping and rising of the deck. But for the bite of the *noroeste,* she would have begun to feel faint and empty in her belly. Now she clutched at the rigging with more courage.

At last the dinghy shoved away, with its first load of passengers — seven boys from Bo-

ngabon, Mindoro, on their way to Manila to
study. The deck seemed less hostile than before, for the boys had made a boisterous group
then; now that they were gone, her mistress
Ana could leave the crowded deckhouse for
once.

"Oh, Elay! My powder puff!"

It was Ana, indeed. Elay was familiar
with that excitement which her mistress wore
about her person like a silk kerchief — now on
her head to keep her hair in place, now like
a scarf round her neck. How eager Ana had
been to go ashore when the old skipper of the
batel said that the *Ligaya* was too small a boat
to brave the coming storm. She must return
to the deckhouse, Elay thought, if she must fetch
her mistress' handbag.

With both hands upon the edge of the deckhouse roof, then holding on to the wooden water
barrel to the left of the main mast, she staggered
back to the deckhouse entrance. As she bent
her head low lest with the lurching of the boat
her brow should hit the door, she saw her mistress on all fours clambering out of the deck-

house. She let her have the right of way, entering only after Ana was safe upon the open deck.

Elay found the handbag — she was certain that the powder puff would be there — though not without difficulty, inside the canvas satchel that she meant to take ashore. She came dragging the heavy satchel, and in a flurry Ana dug into it for the bag. The deck continued to sway, yet presently Ana was powdering her face; and this done, she applied lipstick to that full round mouth of hers.

The wind began to press Elay's blouse against her breasts while she waited on her mistress patiently. She laced Ana's shoes and also bestirred herself to see that Ana's earrings were not askew. For Ana must appear every inch the dressmaker that she was. Let everyone know that she was traveling to Manila — not just to the provincial capital; and, of course, there was the old spinster aunt, too, for company — to set up a shop in the big city. It occurred to Elay that, judging from the care her mistress was taking to look well, it might well be that they were not on board a one-masted Tingloy batel with a cargo of lumber, copra, pigs, and chickens, but were still at home in the dress shop that they were leaving behind in the lumber town of Sumagui.

"How miserable I'd be without you, Elay," Ana giggled, as though somewhere she was meeting a secret lover who for certain would hold her in his arms in one wild passionate caress.

And thinking so of her mistress made Elay more proud of her. She did not mind the dark world into which they were going. Five miles to the south was Pinamalayan town; its lights blinked faintly at her. Then along the rim of the Bay, dense groves of coconuts and underbrush stood, occasional fires marking where the few sharecroppers of the district lived. The batel had anchored at the northernmost end of the cove and apparently five hundred yards from the boat was the palm-leaf-covered hut the old skipper of the *Ligaya* had spoken about.

"Do you see it? That's Obregano's hut." And Obregano, the old skipper explained, was a fisherman. The men who sailed up and down the eastern coast of Mindoro knew him well. There was not a seaman who lived in these parts but had gone to Obregano for food or shelter and to this anchorage behind the northern tip of Pinamalayan Bay for the protection it offered sailing vessels against the unpredictable *noroeste*.

The old skipper had explained all this to Ana, and Elay had listened, little knowing that in a short while it would all be there before her. Now in the dark she saw the fisherman's hut readily. A broad shoulder of a hill rose beyond, and farther yet the black sky looked like a silent wall.

Other women joined them on the deck to see the view for themselves. A discussion started; some members of the party did not think that it would be proper for them to spend the night in Obregano's hut. Besides the students, there were four middle-aged merchants on this voyage; since Bongabon they had plagued the women with their coarse talk and their yet coarser laughter. Although the deckhouse was the unchallenged domain of the women, the four middle-aged merchants had often slipped in, and once inside had exchanged lewd jokes among themselves, to the embarrassment of their audience. Small wonder, Elay thought, that the prospect of spending the night in a small fisherman's hut and with these men for company did not appear attractive to the other women passengers. Her mistress Ana had made up her mind, however. She had a sense of independence that Elay admired.

Already the old aunt had joined them on deck; and Elay said to herself, "Of course, it's for this old auntie's sake, too. She has been terribly seasick."

In the dark she saw the dinghy and silently watched it being sculled back to the batel. It drew nearer and nearer, a dark mass moving eagerly, the bow pointing in her direction. Elay heard Ana's little shrill cries of excitement. Soon two members of the crew were vying for the honor of helping her mistress safely into the dinghy.

Oh, that Ana should allow herself to be thus honored, with the seamen taking such pleasure from it all, and the old aunt, watching, pouting her lips in disapproval! "What shall I do?" Elay asked herself, anticipating that soon she herself would be the object of this chivalrous byplay. And what could the old aunt be saying now to herself? "Ah, women these days are no longer decorous. In no time they will make a virtue of being unchaste."

Elay pouted, too. And then it was her turn. She must get into that dinghy, and it so pitched and rocked. If only she could manage to have no one help her at all. But she'd fall into the water. Santa Maria. I'm safe....

They were off. The waves broke against the sides of the dinghy, threatening to capsize it, and continually the black depths glared at her. Her hands trembling, Elay clung tenaciously to the gunwale. Spray bathed her cheeks. A boy began to bail, for after clearing each wave the dinghy took in more water. So earnest was the boy at this chore that Elay thought the boat had sprung a leak and would sink any moment.

The sailors, one at the prow and the other busy with the oar at the stern, engaged themselves in senseless banter. Were they trying to make light of the danger? She said her prayers as the boat swung from side to side, to a rhythm set by the sailor with the oar.

Fortunately, panic did not seize her. It was the old aunt who cried "Susmariosep!" For with each crash of waves, the dinghy lurched precipitously. "God spare us all!" the old aunt prayed frantically.

And Ana was laughing. "Auntie! Why, Auntie, it's nothing! It's nothing at all!" For, really, they were safe. The dinghy had struck sand.

Elay's dread of the water suddenly vanished and she said to herself: "Ah, the old aunt is only making things more difficult for herself." Why, she wouldn't let the sailor with the oar lift her clear of the dinghy and carry her to the beach!

"Age before beauty," the sailor was saying to his companion. The other fellow, not to be outdone, had jumped waist-deep into the water, saying: "No, beauty above all!" Then there was Ana stepping straight, as it were, into the sailor's arms.

"Where are you?" the old aunt was calling from the shore. "Are you safe? Are you all right?"

Elay wanted to say that in so far as she was concerned she was safe, she was all right. She couldn't speak for her mistress, of course! But the same seaman who had lifted the old aunt and carried her to the shore in his arms had returned. Now he stood before Elay and caught her two legs and let them rest on his forearm and then held her body up, with the other arm. Now she was clear of the dinghy, and she had to hold on to his neck. Then the sailor made three quick steps toward dry sand and then let her slide easily off his arms, and she said: "I am all right. Thank you."

Instead of saying something to her the sailor hurried away, joining the group of students that had gathered up the rise of sand. Ana's cheerful laughter rang in their midst. Then a youth's voice, clear in the wind: "Let's hurry to the fisherman's hut!"

A drizzle began to fall. Elay took a few tentative steps toward the palm-leaf hut, but her knees were unsteady. The world seemed to turn and turn, and the glowing light at the fisherman's door swung as from a boat's mast. Elay hurried as best she could after Ana and her old aunt, both of whom had already reached the hut. It was only on hearing her name that that weak, unsteady feeling in her knees disappeared.

"Elay—" It was her mistress, of course. Ana was standing outside the door, waiting. "My lipstick, Elay!"

An old man stood at the door of the hut. "I am Obregano, at your service," he said in welcome. "This is my home."

He spoke in a sing-song that rather matched his wizened face. Pointing at a little woman pottering about the stovebox at one end of the one-room hut, he said: "And she? Well, the guardian of my home — in other words, my wife!"

The woman got up and welcomed them, beaming a big smile. "Feel at home. Make yourselves comfortable — everyone."

She helped Elay with the canvas bag, choosing a special corner for it. "It will rain harder yet tonight, but here your bag will be safe," the woman said.

The storm had come. The thatched wall shook, producing a weird skittering sound at each gust of wind. The sough of the palms in back of the hut — which was hardly the size of the deckhouse of the batel, and had the bare sand for floor — sounded like the moan of a lost child. A palm leaf that served to cover an entrance to the left of the stovebox began to dance a mad, rhythmless dance. The fire in the stove leaped intermittently, rising beyond the lid of the kettle that Obregano the old fisherman had placed there.

And yet the hut was homelike. It was warm and clean. There was a cheerful look all over the place. Elay caught the old fisherman's smile as his wife cleared the floor of blankets, nets, and coil after coil of hempen rope

so that their guests could have more room. She
sensed an affinity with her present surround-
ings, with the smell of the fish nets, with the
dancing fire in the stovebox. It was as though
she had lived in this hut before. She remembered what Obregano's wife had said to her.
The old woman's words were by far the kind-
est she had heard in a long time.

The students from Bongabon had appro-
priated a corner for themselves and begun to
discuss supper. It appeared that a prankster
had relieved one of the chicken coops of a fat
pullet and a boy asked the fisherman for permission to prepare a stew.

"I've some ginger tea in the kettle," Obregano said. "Something worth drinking in
weather like this." He asked his wife for an
old enameled tin cup for their guests to drink
from.

As the cup was being passed around, Obregano's wife expressed profuse apologies for her
not preparing supper. "We have no food," she
said with uncommon frankness. "We have sons,
you know; two of them, both working in town.

But they come home only on week ends. It is only then that we have rice."

Elay understood that in lieu of wages the two Obregano boys received rice. Last week end the boys had failed to return home, however. This fact brought a sad note to Elay's new world of warm fire and familiar smells. She got out some food which they had brought along from the boat — *adobo* and bread that the old aunt had put in a tin container and tucked into the canvas satchel — and offered her mistress these, going through the motions so absent-mindedly that Ana chided her.

"Do offer the old man and his wife some of that, too."

Obregano shook his head. He explained that he would not think of partaking of the food — so hungry his guests must be. They needed all the food themselves, to say nothing about that which his house should offer but which in his naked poverty he could not provide. But at least they would be safe here for the night, Obregano assured them. "The wind is rising,

and the rain too... Listen...." He pointed at
the roof, which seemed to sag.

The drone of the rain set Elay's spirits
aright. She began to imagine how sad and
worried over her sons the old fisherman's wife
must be, and how lonely — but oh how lovely!
— it would be to live in this God-forsaken spot.
She watched the students devour their supper,
and she smiled thanks, sharing their thought-
fulness, when they offered most generously some
chicken to Ana and, in sheer politeness, to the
old spinster aunt also.

Yet more people from the batel arrived,
and the four merchants burst into the hut dis-
cussing some problem in Bongabon municipal
politics. It was as though the foul weather
suited their purposes, and Elay listened with
genuine interest, with compassion, even, for the
small-town politicians who were being reviled
and cursed.

It was Obregano who suggested that they
all retire. There was hardly room for everyone, and in bringing out a rough-woven palm-
leaf mat for Ana and her companions to use,

Obregano picked his way in order not to step on a sprawling leg or an outstretched arm. The offer of the mat touched Elay's heart, so much so that pondering the goodness of the old fisherman and his wife took her mind away from the riddles which the students at this time were exchanging among themselves. They were funny riddles and there was much laughter. Once she caught them throwing glances in Ana's direction.

Even the sailors who were with them on the dinghy had returned to the hut to stay and were laughing heartily at their own stories. Elay watched Obregano produce a bottle of kerosene for the lantern, and then hang the lantern with a string from the center beam of the hut. She felt a new dreamlike joy. Watching the old fisherman's wife extinguish the fire in the stove made Elay's heart throb.

Would the wind and the rain worsen? The walls of the hut shook — like a man in the throes of malaria chills. The sea kept up a wild roar, and the waves, it seemed, continually clawed at the land with strong, greedy fingers.

She wondered whether Obregano and his wife would ever sleep. The couple would be thinking: "Are our guests comfortable enough as they are?" As for herself, Elay resolved, she would stay awake. From the corner where the students slept she could hear the whine of a chronic asthma sufferer. One of the merchants snorted periodically, like a horse being plagued by a fly. A young boy, apparently dreaming, called out in a strange, frightened voice: "No, no! I can't do that! I wouldn't do that!"

She saw Obregano get up and pick his way again among the sleeping bodies to where the lantern hung. The flame was sputtering. Elay watched him adjust the wick of the lantern and give the oil container a gentle shake. Then the figure of the old fisherman began to blur and she could hardly keep her eyes open. A soothing tiredness possessed her. As she yielded easily to sleep, with Ana to her left and the old spinster aunt at the far edge of the mat to her right, the floor seemed to sink and the walls of the hut to vanish, as though the world were one vast dark valley.

When later she awoke she was trembling with fright. She had only a faint notion that she had screamed. What blur there had been in her consciousness before falling asleep was as nothing compared with that which followed her waking, although she was aware of much to-do and the lantern light was gone.

"Who was it?" It was reassuring to hear Obregano's voice.

"The lantern, please!" That was Ana, her voice shrill and wiry.

Elay heard as if in reply the crash of the sea rising in a crescendo. The blur lifted a little: "Had I fallen asleep after all? Then it must be past midnight by now." Time and place became realities again; and she saw Obregano, with a lighted matchstick in his hand. He was standing in the middle of the hut.

"What happened?"

Elay thought that it was she whom Obregano was speaking to. She was on the point of answering, although she had no idea of what to say, when Ana, sitting up on the mat beside her, blurted out: "Someone was here. Please hold up the light."

"Someone was here," Elay repeated to herself and hid her face behind Ana's shoulder. She must not let the four merchants, nor the students either, stare at her so. Caught by the lantern light, the men hardly seven steps away had turned their gazes upon her in various attitudes of amazement.

Everyone seemed eager to say something all at once. One of the students spoke in a quavering voice, declaring that he had not moved where he lay. Another said he had been so sound asleep — "Didn't you hear me snoring?" he asked a companion, slapping him on the back — he had not even heard the shout. One of the merchants hemmed and suggested that perhaps cool minds should look into the case, carefully and without preconceived ideas. To begin with, one must know exactly what happened. He looked in Ana's direction and said: "Now please tell us."

Elay clutched her mistress' arm. Before Ana could speak, Obregano's wife said: "This thing ought not to have happened. If only our two sons were home, they'd avenge the honor of our house." She spoke with a rare eloquence for an angry woman. "No one would then dare think of so base an act. Now, our good guests," she added, addressing her husband, bitterly, "why, they know you to be an aged, simple-hearted fisherman — nothing more. The good name of your home, of our family, is no concern of theirs."

"Evil was coming, I knew it!" said the old spinster aunt; and piping out like a bird: "Let us return to the boat! Don't be so bitter, old one," she told Obregano's wife. "We are going back to the boat."

"It was like this," Ana said, not minding her aunt. Elay lowered her head more, lest she should see those man-faces before her, loosely trapped now by the lantern's glow. Indeed, she closed her eyes, as though she were a little child afraid of the dark.

"It was like this," her mistress began again, "I was sleeping, and then my maid, Elay—" she put an arm around Elay's shoulder — "she uttered that wild scream. I am surprised you did not hear it."

In a matter-of-fact tone, one of the merchants countered: "Suppose it was a nightmare?"

But Ana did not listen to him. "Then my maid," she continued, "this girl here — she's hardly twenty, mind you, and an innocent and illiterate girl, if you must all know.... She turned round, trembling, and clung to me...."

"Couldn't she possibly have shouted in her sleep?" the merchant insisted.

Obregano had held his peace all this time, but now he spoke: "Let us hear what the girl says."

And so kind were those words! How fatherly of him to have spoken so, in such a gentle and understanding way! Elay's heart went to him. She felt she could almost run to him and, crying over his shoulders, tell him what no one, not even Ana herself, would ever know.

She turned her head a little to one side and saw that now they were all looking at her.

She hugged her mistress tighter, in a childlike embrace, hiding her face as best she could.

"Tell them," Ana said, drawing herself away. "Now, go on — speak!"

But Elay would not leave her side. She clung to her, and began to cry softly.

"Nonsense!" the old aunt chided her.

"Well, she must have had a nightmare, that's all," the merchant said, chuckling. "I'm sure of it!"

At this remark Elay cried even more. "I felt a warm hand caressing my — my — my cheeks," she said, sobbing. "A warm hand, I swear," she said again, remembering how it had reached out for her in the dark, searchingly, burning with a need to find some precious treasure which, she was certain of it now, she alone possessed. For how could it be that they should force her to tell them? "Someone," — the word was like a lamp in her heart — "someone wanted me," she said to herself.

She felt Ana's hand stroking her back ungently and then heard her saying, "I brought this on," then nervously fumbling about the mat. "This is all my fault.... My compact, please...."

But Elay was inconsolable. She was sorry she could be of no help to her mistress now. She hung her head, unable to stop her tears from cleansing those cheeks that a warm hand had loved.

THE SEA BEYOND

T HE *Adela,* the reconverted minesweeper
that had become the mainstay of com-
merce and progress in Sipolog Oriental, was on
her way to San Roque. As Horacio Arenas,
our new assistant, wanted to put it, the *Adela*
was "expected" at San Roque, which was the
provincial capital, "in seven hours." He spoke
at some length of this particular voyage, looking
worn-out instead of refreshed after the two-week
vacation we had hoped he would enjoy.

There he was, he said, one of the hundred odd impatient passengers that shivered under the low canvas awning of the upper deck. A choppy sea met the ship as she approached Punta Dumadáli, and the rise and fall of the deck suggested the labored breathing of an already much-abused beast of burden. Her hatches were in fact quite full, Arenas said. Hundreds of sacks of copra had filled her hold at Dias. Piled all over the lower deck were thousands of pieces of lauan boards from the mills of San Tomé. The passageways alongside the engine room were blocked by enormous baskets of cassava and bananas. A dozen wild-eyed Simara cows, shoulder to shoulder in their makeshift corral at the stern, mooed intermittently as though the moon-drenched sea were their pasture.

For the moon had risen over the Maniwala Ranges three miles to the starboard. As more and more the *Adela* rounded the Punta Dumadáli, the wind sent the ship bucking wildly. An hour before, all this would have been understandable; it was puzzling, if not thoroughly incomprehensible now. This kind of sea was un-

usual for the reason that the Dumadáli head-
land was known to mariners to throw off, especially this time of the year if at no other, the
full force of the *noroeste*. If some explanation
were to sought, it would be in some circumstance
peculiar only to this voyage. This was the con-
census, which made possible the next thought:
that some presence was about, some evil force
perhaps — so the talk went on board — which,
until propitiated, might yet bring the ship to
some foul end. The cows, so insistent in their
lowing before, were markedly quiet now. The
ship continued to pitch about; whenever the
wind managed to tear at the awnings and cause
loose ends of canvas to beat savagely at the wire-
mesh that covered the railings, small unreal
patches of sea glimmered outside in the moon-
light.

It was no secret that there was a dying man
on board. He was out there in the third-class
section. Whatever relation his presence had to
the unpleasantness in the weather no one could
explain, but the captain did do something. He
had the man moved over to the first-class sec-

tion, where there were fewer passengers and where it was perhaps more comfortable.

The transfer was accomplished by two members of the crew. They carried the cot in which the man lay, and two women, the man's wife and her mother, followed them. Ample space was cleared for the cot; the two women helped push the heavy canvas beds and chairs out of the way. Finally the two men brought the canvas cot down. The ship listed to the starboard suddenly; and it seemed that from all quarters of the deck the hundred odd passengers of the *Adela* let out a wild scream.

Then the ship steadied somehow. For a moment it seemed as if her engines had stopped. Then there was a gentle splashing sound as though the bow had clipped neatly through the last of those treacherous waves. Either superior seamanship or luck held sway, but the ship might have entered then an estuary, perhaps the very mouth of a river.

The excitement had roused the passengers and, in the first-class section at least, everyone had sat up to talk, to make real all over again the danger they had just been through. The steaming-hot coffee which the steward began serving in thick blue-rimmed cups encouraged conversation. The presence of the two women and the man in the extra cot in their midst was hardly to be overlooked. A thick grey woolen blanket covered the man all over, except about the face. His groans underscored by the faint tapping of the wind on the canvas awnings were becoming all too familiar. The mother attracted some notice, although for a different reason; she had a particularly sharp-edged face — brow and nose and chin had a honed look to them. The wife, who had more pleasing features, evoked respect and compassion. It was touching to see her sit on the edge of the empty cot beside her husband's and tuck in the hem of her skirt under her knees. She could not have been more than twenty, and already she wore the sadness of her widowhood. The glare of the naked electric bulb that hung from the ridge-pole of the deck's canvas roof accentuated it, revealed that she was about six months gone with child, and called attention to her already full breasts, under a rust-colored camisa, that soon would be nourishing yet another life.

It was four hours before, at Dias, where the accident had occurred. Although Dias was a rich port, no wharf had been constructed either by the government or the local association of copra and rice merchants. The old method of ferrying cargo in small outriggered paraos was less costly perhaps; it was even picturesque. But it was only possible in good weather. And already the noroeste had come. The same waves that pounded at the side of the *Adela* at anchor lashed at the frail paraos that were rowed over toward the ship and were brought into position for hauling up the copra. The man, one of the cargadores, had fallen off the ship's side.

He would have gone to the bottom had he not let go of the copra sack that he had held aloft, and more so had he not been caught across the hips by the outriggers of his parao. Nonetheless, the next wave that lifted the ship and gathered strength from under her keel it seemed flung him headlong toward the prow of the boat. The blunt end of this dugout pressed his body against the black, tar-coated side of the *Adela*. The crew pulled him out with difficulty, for the sea kept rising and falling and caused the prow's head to scrape continuously against the ship's side. The crew had expected to find a mass of broken flesh and bones, but in actuality the man came through quite intact. He did not start moaning and writhing until his wet undershirt and shorts had been changed and he had been laid out on the cot. There was nothing that could be done further except to keep him on board. Something after all had broken or had burst open somewhere inside him.

His family was sent for. The wife, accompanied by her mother, clambered up the ship's side thirty minutes later, to the jocose shouts of "Now you can see San Roque!" from innocent well-wishers in the paraos. The shippers, the Dias Development Co., had sent a telegram to the provincial doctor at San Roque, and an agent of the company had come on board and personally commended the cargador to the captain. When at last the fifty-ton copra shipment was on board, the *Adela* weighed anchor.

Now for having transferred the man from the third-class to the first-class section, the captain earned some praise and the connection between this act and the pleasant change in the weather elicited much speculation. If only the man did not groan so pitifully, if only he kept his misery to himself; if only the two women were less preoccuppied too by some bitter and long-unresolved conflict between them. "Don't you think he is hungry?" the mother once asked; to which the wife answered, "He does not like food. You know that." And then the mother asked, "How about water? He will be thirsty perhaps;" and the wife's reply was, "I shall go down and fetch some water." The matter could have stopped there, but the mother wanted to have the last word. "That's better than just standing or sitting around."

The wife got up and walked away, only to return about ten minutes later with a pitcher and a drinking cup from the mess room below. The mother had the pitcher and drinking cup placed at the foot of the sick man's bed, for, as she explained, "He will ask for water any time and you won't be near enough to help me." The mother waited to see what her daughter would make of this; and the latter did have her say: "I'll be right here, Mother, if that's all you're worried about."

The man grew restless. His wife's assurance (she said again and again, "You will be all right!") drew nothing but interminable sighs ("Oh, God of mine!"). Between the man and his wife, some inexplicable source of irritation had begun to fester. "It is in your trying to move about that the pain comes," the wife chided him gently. "We are getting there soon. It will not be long now." Whereupon the man tried to raise his knee and twist his hips under the blanket. The blanket made a hump like one of the Maniwala mountains in the distance, and he let out a wail, followed by "But this boat is so very slow, God of mine! Why can't we go faster? Let the captain make the boat go faster. Tell him. Will someone go and tell him?"

Almost breathless after this exertion, he lay still. The mother, this time as if her son-in-law were an ally, took it upon herself to comfort him. "Better keep quiet and don't tire yourself. The captain will make the boat go faster, surely." And by putting down his knee carefully, the hump that the blanket had made before leveled off now into foothills instead of those high ranges of the Maniwala.

The business of the telegram came after this lull. It was preceded by a prolonged groan, and then the question was there before them: "And did they send the telegram?" "They" meant the Company of course, in whose service the man had enlisted as a cargador. If the answer to this was in the affirmative, then there was reason to say that the doctor would attend to him and put him together again and return him to his work. His wife assured him that the telegram had gone. "So now be quiet," she added. "The other people here would not want to be disturbed now. They want to sleep, no doubt," she said, looking round her, seeking the faces of some twenty or twenty-five passengers

— which included merchants, students, and at least three public schoolteachers on some Christmas holiday jaunt.

The mother asked about food — a proper question, although under the circumstances perhaps a tactless one. "I am not hungry, Mother," was what the daughter said, firmly. "I'll sit here," the mother offered, in a less authoritative tone than she had been accustomed to use. "I'll do that myself if you are hungry," countered the daughter. "I don't care for food," the mother assured her. "And did I tell you I wanted to eat?" Whereupon the daughter declared that she was not hungry, "—let me tell you that, Mother." The mother alleged that her most loving daughter was no doubt "too choosy" about food, "that's why." She ought to "go down below and ask for anything to eat." "Eat whatever you can find," was her solemn injunction, as if to overwhelm her daughter's claim that she was not hungry at all. "Don't worry about me, Mother," the wife added, pointedly. "I don't get hungry that easily." And then to round off this phase of their quarrel, the mother said, loud enough for anyone who cared to hear: "Maybe, it's sitting at the captain's table that you've been waiting for all this time."

The daughter said nothing in reply and the mother did not press her advantage either. It was clear, though, that the meaning of the remark, its insinuation, was not to be easily dismissed. What the mother had so expressed was a little out of the ordinary; the air, as Arenas put it, was rife with conjectures. It was not difficult to remember, he said, that ship officers, or sailors in general, had never been known to endow women their highest value. What remained to be understood was why the mother thought of her daughter in some such awful connection as this.

Five hours later, Arenas said, after the *Adela* had docked at the San Roque pier and the discharging of some of her cargo had begun, the subject came up again. Perhaps the first person to disembark had been the captain himself, to infer from the fact that somebody, possibly one of the mates, had shouted to some one standing on the wharf: "Duty before pleasure, captain!" A jeep of the Southern Star Navigation Co. had rolled up the ramp and then hurried off the mile-long seaside road toward the town, into San Roque *poblacion* itself. The town was brightly lighted, particularly the section along the seaside.

"Now he's gone and we have not even thanked him," said the mother. "And the doctor has not come. How can we leave this ship? Answer that," she demanded. "You are too proud, that's what. All that you needed to say was a word or two, a word of thanks, surely." The wife remained silent through all this. "And he could have taken you in the jeep, to fetch the doctor; if there was that telegram, and it has been received—" She did not go further. The wife assured her calmly that the telegram was sent. "So what harm could it have done to have spoken to the captain, to have reminded him, since he would be riding into town anyway?" the mother said; and to this the daughter's reply was the kind of serenity, Arenas said, that can come only from knowledge: "All men know is to take advantage of us, Mother," she said.

Taken aback by these words, the mother searched the faces of people round her for help. She got nothing and she said nothing. The passengers had crowded at the railing to watch the lumber being unloaded. A gang of carga-dores tossed pieces of lumber from over the ship's side to the wharf ten feet away while someone chanted: "A hundred and fifty-three- and fifty-four- and fifty-five...." and the wood cluttered askew on the fast-mounting pile. The cows lowed again from their corral at the stern of the ship. This blended afresh with the man's groans and with the chant and the clatter of the boards. Meanwhile, the wife talked on softly: "We have arrived, and it's the doctor's jeep we're waiting for and nothing more," wiping her husband's brow with a hand-kerchief. "Two hundred and three — and four — and five...." chanted the counter, over down below. "This is San Roque now," the wife continued. "A big town it is, with many lights. And with many people." Her husband's brow sweated profusely and it was all she could do with her handkerchief. "And the lights are bright, and so many. Rest now and tomorrow we can see the town," she said softly, folding her handkerchief this way and that so as not to get any section of it too damp with sweat.

It was at this point, Arenas said, that a motor sounded from down the road, followed by the blare of a jeep's horn and the swing of its headlights. The lights caught the man who was chanting his count of the lumber being unloaded, and they held him transfixed. He shouted out the numbers louder. The jeep stopped in the middle of the now cluttered up wharf, for what with the stacked rows of copra and the lauan boards from San Tomé there was no space for the jeep to move in. The driver, having gone no farther than possible, turned off his engine and slid off his seat awkwardly, and then approaching the man who was doing the counting, he demanded: "How much longer?" And the other replied: "Possibly until two o'clock—what with the men we have. You know how it is, sir." To which the other said, sternly: "Stop calling me 'sir'. And to think that the captain just told me he'll pull out in two hours, not a second later."

Words, Arenas said, which, although intended for somebody else did make the wife say to her husband: "They'll first move you over there, to the wharf — that will be solid ground at least — and there we shall wait for the doctor." She had dropped her voice to a whisper.

Across the ten feet of water to the edge of the wharf, lights fell harshly on the piles, on the heads and arms of the cargadores who slid up and down the gangplank with the copra sacks on their shoulders, looking like so many over-sized ants. To the right was the driver in his jeep; he had not turned off his lights and it flooded the first-class section with a garish glare. "What shamelessness," cried the wife. The jeep's lights singled her out. The driver had got stuck between the wall of copra to his left and a new pile of lumber to his right. He was trying to turn the jeep about but did not have the room. The man who had addressed him "Sir" had stopped his work, and the clatter of the boards had ceased. Up on the deck, Arenas said, the wife shouted: "What does he want of me? What does he want me to do now?" The mother pulled her away. "She's overwrought. Forgive her," she begged. "And as you've observed, I've been hard on her myself. I don't know why. Why must God punish us so?"

Once more the driver tried to manuever his jeep and all the time his lights seemed to fix themselves forever on the wife, who, to meet this challenge, sprang away from the ship's railing and rushed down to the lower deck, shouting: "Here, here I am. Take me. What can you want of me?"

It was that way, Arenas said. Two hours later, the man was moved to the wharf, and there behind a pile of copra and another pile of lauan lumber the wife and the mother waited. Word was abroad that the captain, who had returned from town, had said that he had contacted the doctor. Contacted, Arenas said, was the very word. And wasn't that so revealing?

We didn't know at first what he meant, we told him. Did he want to remind us about the war, the same one during which the *Adela* had swept the mine-strewn sea in behalf of progress and civilization? The word Arenas had used belonged to that time, and he seemed to say, All this because it had been that way at that time. You must understand, you might forgive, even.

But we didn't want him to be apologetic like the mother-in-law he had described; and so, afterward, when he talked again about the subject, wearing that worried look on his face with which we had become familiar, we had to urge him: "Better not think about it any more."

COME AND GO

ONE MORNING in October 1940, Felipe (alias Philip) Bautista, thirty-six, steward third class, U.S. Naval Transport Service, arrived in Buenavista on the Nuestra Señora del Carmen for a brief visit with his family. He had neither written nor sent a wire. It was as if he had done so on purpose. To Nanay, letters had somehow meant serious money troubles; telegrams had never been anything but ruthless messengers of death. With a notice from the North American Life Assurance Co., of Toronto, in her hand, she once dragged her slippers all over town, seeking out her relatives and friends for counsel; for she could not quite bring herself to believe that anyone in the world could possibly have the kindness to offer her two thousand pesos just because Papa had died. Yet that was exactly what the letter had said, and she had walked home with a heavy heart, shaking her head, unable to comprehend the disguises of Providence.

Philip had not found this amusing at all, although in a quite longish letter of Perla's that had reached him in San Francisco, she had said that it was. Nanay was now five years dead, Philip told himself. It was pointless to ask what she would say about this visit, but he couldn't help thinking of her. Surely, were she alive, she would wish he had brought along some presents for the family.

Unfortunately, he had bought his ticket on an impulse; and realizing that he had no time to shop, he did not even try to get a bag or two of oranges and mangoes from the rowdy fruit peddlers at the pier. The family would understand, he had hoped; and by family Philip meant merely his sister Perla, whom he had not seen in thirteen years, and her husband, whom he knew only by name.

He had not expected any one to meet him at the wharf and, though the crowd was large and the air rang with suddenly familar greetings in Bisayan, he did find no one there to welcome him. He reminded himself that there were but ninety tons of copra to load up from the Stevenson warehouse; for this he might allow two hours. Promptly afterward, he figured, the ship would weigh anchor for the return voyage to Manila.

A short walk across the town plaza and past the market place, and he was home. And this then was Perla, the "Perls" of those letters he had posted from such odd places as Baltimore, Port Niches, and Vancouver. She had run up to the porch, crying, "Oh, *manong,* you almost scared me!" — and what with the children there gathered about her, she looked like Nanay all over, the Nanay of long ago, before he had put the two poles of the earth between them.

"This must be Rebby," he said, holding the feet of the baby that Perls carried astride her hip, exactly as Nanay in her day might carry around a ten-month-old. "Did I scare you also, Rebby?" he asked. Her feet were the softest things his hands had held in a long time.

Jerking her legs, Rebby gave out a shrill, tremulous cry. "But it's your Uncle Philip!" said Perls and, turning to him, explained: "She's just now cutting her teeth. That's why she's so bad-tempered.... And this is Sid," she added, pulling gently from behind her the little girl who had been clinging to the Mother Hubbard that made Perls look like a long-widowed fishwife. "You be quiet, you!" she threatened, slapping Rebby on the thigh. "You've come on the Carmen? It's already six. My, we must have breakfast soon. Ruuuddy! Ruuuuuuddd-dyyy!" she called. But no one answered. "He must have gone to buy the bread already. That boy minds his chores."

So this is the family: the thought kept coming like a refrain. And this the house: a three-room frame house set on the side of the rock-covered hill overlooking the harbor. Here it was, complete with the strip of gravelled road before it and the embankment that kept the sea away at high tide. The porch, not yet washed dry by the morning sunshine, had the dank odor that exuded from those rocks and the sour-sop trees in the yard.

Perls led the way into the *sala* and opened the windows that framed in each of them a view of the wharf and the interisland steamer moored alongside. Beside the Stevenson warehouse rose the hill of copra from where a hundred stevedores or so, like hungry ants blessed with a pile of sugar, hurried off to the ship, the brown sacks on their sweat-soaked and glistening bodies.

Philip wanted to enjoy the scene, for it recalled something from his boyhood. But Perls wanted to show him the room where Papa and Nanay had died. The four-poster with its sagging bejuco weave, except perhaps for the torn sheet that Rudy had slipped out of, was exactly as Philip had seen it last. On the floor was a *buri* mat over which a green-and-red checkered mosquito bar hung: here, then, Perls and the two children slept. She had dragged out Rebby and Sid from here to see who had been pounding at the door.

"I didn't recognize your voice," Perls con-
fessed, laughing. "Fermin — that's my husband
— is with us only three nights of the week. I
thought you were somebody sent over from
Agsawa to bring bad news."

"And what does he do in Agsawa? That's
on the other side of the island, isn't it?"

"That's where he teaches. He's been ban-
ished, you know. And he has not been well.
Asthma. Perhaps worsened by his going up and
down the steep mountain road."

"I hope he gets better," Philip said, feeling suddenly injured and angry even at how
luck had cheated his sister. She ought to have
found somehow a healthier man for a husband.
That would have been a relief at least. Philip
had no idea of how this fellow Fermin looked,
never having seen even a picture of him. The
name itself didn't sound right; Philip imagined
a thin long-necked creature of forty making a
whiz in his throat with each gulp of rain-fresh
mountain air.

"Friday night he's here. It's a three-hour
hike. Then he's back early Monday morning."

"That's difficult," Philip said.

"We can't join him because Rudy's in Grade Six now. Besides, somebody has to stay in this house."

"Perhaps, things will turn out right in the end," Philip said, lamely. He had taken off his gabardine jacket and hung it on the back of the old rattan chair.

"I hope so," Perls said.

"And how old are you, Sid?" Philip asked his niece, telling himself: You can't bear the children any grudges. You mustn't, anyway.

"Six," the girl declared, in English.

"You're in school already? Which grade?"

"Two," the girl said, holding up two fingers of her right hand.

"Rebby's really fourteen months now," Perls said. "You will stay till Saturday, maybe? That's three days at least."

"I can't" said Philip. "I must be back, on that boat over there," and he pointed to the Carmen quietly sitting at the wharf.

"Then you'll not meet him — Fermin, I mean."

"I'm sorry."

"You can't stay, really?"

"I have to be back on my ship by tomorrow evening. I'm lucky enough to have this leave."

"Why, will there be war? People here talk a lot about it," Perls said. "That's why I keep telling my husband, 'Don't feel so bad about things. This is not yet the worst,' I say to him."

"Maybe, you're right," Philip admitted.

"But we'll be safe here? What do you think?" Perls said, nervously. Philip noticed she kept patting Rebby on the back, perhaps to conceal her anxiety.

"You shouldn't worry," said Philip.

"The war will be far away?"

"Maybe," Philip began, but decided not to continue. The transport, USNS Harold Tilyard Matson, had brought fresh units of the 61st Infantry to Manila, but he couldn't tell his sister that. He had expected her to ask: What then? What will happen? Will you be safe? But Perls was doubtless wrapped up in her own small troubles. Husband away in some God-forsaken station, and with asthma and all that. Rebby undernourished. Rudy and Sid to keep in school. Old house to look after. He understood the facts, but something rankled inside him. The name Fermin — that was it! It grated in his ears.

A strange mood prodded his thoughts back to those days when he had begged Papa and Nanay permission to go to America. It pained him to remember the trouble he had caused. Winning Nanay over had been difficult. In his desperation, he had resorted to acting like a blackguard in high school, picking fights, insulting the history teacher, openly challenging the principal to a nine-round boxing bout. From all the trouble he had caused, it became quite clear that as a growing disgrace to the family he ought to be away and out of sight.

Raising the money for his fare had not been easy either. It had to be steerage, but even then Papa had to mortgage his five-hectare coconut grove in Bankalanan. It was three years later that Papa died, and to Philip was sent half of the insurance money so that he might return home. The question had not been, Return home to what? but, rather, with what? A year in Hawaii, two summers in Alaska, and, in between, dreary months in the farms of Fresno. His pride told him he could not go back with only stories about the pool rooms in Sacramento for the folks. Nor would they be satisfied with even the choicest secrets of the *sikoy-sikoy* joints of San Francisco.

He wrote fewer and fewer letters. It was only after Nanay's death, he remembered, that he had hit on the nickname Perls. A correspondence began which, if desultory, took account of Fermin and the children, one after another as they came. In some way all of them became, for Philip, more than ten thousand miles away, somewhat real people.

"Come, Sid. Sit here by me," he called to the little girl and made room for her on the chair.

But she drew away. Philip noticed for the

first time the dress she wore; it looked like an undershirt that her brother had discarded five years before.

"It's your own Uncle Philip, Sid," her mother reminded the girl.

"Let me give you five dollars," he said, pulling out his wallet. He flicked the crisp note before handing it to the girl. "Buy yourself a dress."

"But Philip!" said Perls. "Maybe you don't have enough yourself."

"Who? Me?" he laughed.

"And what do you say to your Uncle Philip?" Perls pressed the girl.

Sid stepped forward but kept her eyes to the floor. "Thank you, Uncle," she said.

"Bright girl! And here's another five dollars for Rebby," said Philip. "Look, Rebby," he said touching the little one's cheek with his forefinger. "Tell Mama to buy a dress also. Now don't you forget."

"They do really need clothes and shoes," said Perls. "The Bankalanan coconuts — we

paid up the mortgage only three years ago—
did not bring in enough last quarter. As for
Fermin's salary—Well, you know how that is."

"What about Mama then? Doesn't Mama
need anything?" He posed the question to both
Rebby and Sid, chuckling, and then looked
into his wallet as if counting the bills in it.
He pulled out and gave Perls a fifty-dollar
note.

"Sid," said Perls, "you better give me
your money. You'll only lose it."

"And Rudy? Whatever happened to Ru-
dy?" Philip asked. He felt expansive, relieved
of those depressing thoughts, even of the re-
sentments, a while back. "It's Rudy I remember very well." He showed Perls the cellophane
leaf in his wallet. "I have been carrying this
snapshot all these years. Look, he has Rebby's
features—the eyes, especially."

Perls looked out the window, craning her
neck in order to see beyond the point where
the embankment turned. "Oh — wait — there
he is now," she said.

Philip took Sid to the window: she was friendly again. He lifted her up so that she could see her brother coming up the road. "Rudy's almost a young man now," Philip said, seeing the barefoot boy with a paper bag in one hand hugged tight to his chest. He was pleased to see that his nephew had his mother's more pleasing features — the oval face, the frank eyes, the full and well-shaped lips.

"Rudy," said Perls, as the boy stopped at the door. "Rudy, do you remember your uncle Philip?"

It was as if the boy was not looking at his mother but at some object beyond. His big round eyes did not blink.

"What have you told him about me?" Philip asked, suddenly vexed.

"Nothing. Nothing much. Except that last year, especially, he kept looking at maps and asking about you. That was when we received your postcard with the picture of your ship."

The reply soothed Philip a little. "Maybe, when he grows up, he'll also . . ."

"Oh, no. God forbid!" Perls gasped.

The boy rubbed the soles of his feet self-consciously on the doorsill. Then he walked into the room as if, to begin with, he did not know what to do with the bag of bread he had bought.

"Let me have it," said his mother. "You look after Rebby. I'll prepare our breakfast."

"You were as big as Rebby when—" but Philip stopped. He was about to tell the boy: —when I first read about you. Instead, he showed him the snapshot in the wallet. "Do you know who that is?"

Rudy shook his head slowly.

"But that's you!" Philip said.

"Me?"

"That's you, of course!"

It was only then that Rudy smiled. He carried Rebby awkwardly and then the baby wet herself; he tried to hold her at arm's length. Philip took Rebby then from him and placed her on his chair.

"She will also wet your chair," said Rudy.

"That's all right," said Philip, keeping Rebby steady. "Tell me, what did your Mama say about me?" he asked softly, quickly.

They could hear Perls in the kitchen. A kettle had crashed to the floor, and the smoke from the woodstove smelled damp. The boy smiled.

"Tell me. What did your Mama say about your uncle Philip?"

"That you were bad."

"What else?"

"That you boxed people's ears and then ran away."

Philip laughed. "Your Mama, of all people!" he said, enjoying himself. "Now, listen, Rudy. You'll come with me to America, will you?" He felt he had to make it up with this boy somehow.

"But I'm too young," Rudy said, his eyes brightening.

"No, not now. When you're older. Look, I'll give you my jacket. Will you try it on?"

The boy fingered the smooth gray fabric, unbelieving, then swung the jacket over his shoulders. It fell very loose down his neck and shoulders. In his short pants and with his bony knees and skinny calves, he looked like a scarecrow out of season.

"Maybe next year, it will fit me," Rudy decided, after looking himself over.

"Good," Philip encouraged him. And here's something else," he said, unfastening the gold watch off his wrist.

"It's for me, really?" Rudy held the bracelet gingerly, afraid that the gold would tarnish at his touch.

"For you," Philip said, now watching the boy wear the timepiece tight up his forearm. "Let's tell Mama all about it."

Rebby could not be kept long on the chair and so Philip had to carry her off.

They had breakfast on the low form in the kitchen. Philip found the board damp and smelly, as though fish broth had been spilled over it and the wood had been soaked all over. He sat on the floor and, having rolled up his shirt-sleeves, dunked his bread in the chocolate that Perls had prepared. It was not as thick as he would have liked; and he saw that the long-necked brass pot Perls used had fallen to the floor, an arm's length from the woodstove. There was a saucerful of crisp anchovies that Perls had roasted in an old frying pan. There was also some fried rice. He was glad Perls had not brought out anything special.

"Rudy has a coat to wear when he goes to America. He has a watch, too," Philip said, halfway through the meal.

"It's your father who needs a watch, Rudy," said Perls from where she sat with Rebby on her lap. Perls fed her with chocolate-dunked bread.

"The jacket doesn't fit him now; but, maybe, later—" Philip began again.

"It's your father who should be wearing things like that, Rudy. He has school programs and meetings to attend. He can use a coat and look better," said his mother.

"I'll let Papa wear it then," Rudy said. "But it still will be mine, won't it?"

"Of course," his uncle said.

"And Papa can use the watch, but it still will be mine," the boy pursued.

"It still will be yours," his uncle said.

"All right, it still will be yours," Perls conceded.

Philip imagined how his jacket would look on his scrawny brother-in-law and wished he had not been so generous to his nephew. He wished the watch would stop ticking the very moment his brother-in-law had it on. He couldn't help asking Perls: "This husband you have, does he take good care of you?"

"How funny you are, Philip," said Perls, putting another piece of bread into Rebby's mouth.

Presently, Rudy got up from the table. Sid followed. Perls was wiping little Rebby's chocolate-smeared face with the hem of the baby's dress when Philip got up and joined his nephew and niece in the *sala*.

"Look," Rudy cried, dancing in circles before his sister Sid. He had put on his uncle's gabardine jacket again. His arms lost in the long sleeves, Rudy dangled the gold watch, teasing his little sister by letting it touch her ears now and then.

"Mine! All mine!" Rudy said, thumping about like some wild little mountain man. Because Rudy would not let Sid listen to the ticking of the watch, the poor girl was almost in tears.

The Carmen let out a sharp hissing sound all of a sudden, followed by four taunting blasts.

"Now we have to hurry," said Perls, running to the bedroom.

After the four blasts, the ship's whistle gave out a long and deep heart-wrenching moan. Rudy looked at his watch.

"Quick, put on your school uniforms," Perls said. She had brought out a little white blouse for Rebby and had changed herself, wearing now a pink, newly-pressed cotton dress with little prints of sailboats at the hem. There would be just enough time to see Philip off. From the wharf, Rudy and Sid would have to hurry off to school.

A thin silver smoke hung over the ship's funnel, lingering there awhile. Philip was entranced by it. It rose in the air slowly transformed into a white silk ribbon, a piece of bunting for the arch of coconuts that crowned the hills beyond across the bay. Then, in a trice, it was gone.

"That's right," Philip said, softly, as if to himself. "I really have to get back."

Vaguely, he saw where Rudy belonged. Then, more clearly: Friday was not too far away—soon the the boy's joys would be over. Already, Perls could count on adding to her fifty dollars the ten from Rebby and Sid. But then all that money would go for clothes, shoes, and the medicines that Fermin—that horrible name!—needed for his asthma. And food, too.

Philip was frightened by his knowledge of Perl's burden, and he was hurt by his own foolish and futile gestures toward making it seem easier to bear. There was the war she feared, and she had forgotten him altogether.

It seemed that his thirteen years of escape from this house had converged upon him for the sole purpose of making him wish Perls all the strength and courage she needed; and he forgave her the chocolate, her exiled spouse, even that horrid Mother Hubbard. It was not inconceivable after all that someday, out there at sea, he would have to go, like that wisp of smoke, and vanish into nowhere.

THE BREAD OF SALT

USUALLY I was in bed by ten and up by
five and thus was ready for one more day
of my fourteenth year. Unless Grandmother had
forgotten, the fifteen centavos for the baker
down Progreso Street—and how I enjoyed jing-
ling those coins in my pocket! — would be in
the empty fruit-jar in the cupboard. I would
remember then that rolls were what Grandmother wanted because recently she had lost
three molars. For young people like my cousins and myself, she had always said that the
kind called *pan de sal* ought to be quite all right.

The bread of salt! How did it get that
name? From where did its flavor come; through
what secret action of flour and yeast? At the
risk of being jostled from the counter by other
early buyers, I would push my way into the
shop so that I might watch the men who, strip-
ped to the waist, worked their long flat wooden

spades in and out of the glowing maw of the
oven. Why did the bread come nut-brown and
the size of my little fist? And why did it have
a pair of lips convulsed into a painful frown?
In the half-light of the street, and hurrying,
the paper bag pressed to my chest, I felt my
curiosity a little gratified by the oven-fresh
warmth of the bread I was proudly bringing
home for breakfast.

Well I knew how Grandmother would not
mind if I nibbled away at one piece; perhaps,
I might even eat two pieces, to be charged later
against my share at the table. But that would
be betraying a trust; and so, indeed, I kept my
purchase intact. To guard it from harm, I
watched my steps and avoided the dark street
corners.

For my reward, I had only to look in the
direction of the sea-wall and the fifty yards
or so of river bed beyond it, where an old Spaniard's house stood. At low tide, when the bed
was dry and the rocks glinted with broken bot-
tles, the stone fence of the Spaniard's compound
set off the house as if it were a castle. Sunrise

brought a wash of silver upon the roof of the laundry and garden sheds which had been built low and close to the fence. On dull mornings the light dripped from the bamboo screen which covered the veranda and hung some four or five yards from the ground. Unless it was August, when the damp northeast monsoon had to be kept away from the rooms, three servants raised the screen promptly at six-thirty until it was completely hidden under the veranda eaves. From the sound of the pulleys I knew it was time to set out for school.

It was in his service, as a coconut plantation overseer, that Grandfather had spent the last thirty years of his life. Grandmother had been widowed three years now. I often wondered whether I was being depended upon to spend the years ahead in the service of this great house. One day I learned that Aida, a classmate in high school, was the old Spaniard's niece. All my doubts disappeared. It was as if before his death Grandfather had spoken to me about her, concealing the seriousness of the matter by putting it over as a joke. If now

I kept true to the virtues, she would step out of her bedroom ostensibly to say Good Morning to her uncle. Her real purpose, I knew, was to reveal thus her assent to my desire.

On quiet mornings I imagined the patter of her shoes upon the wooden veranda floor as a further sign, and I would hurry off to school, taking the route she had fixed for me past the post office, the town plaza and the church, the health center east of the plaza, and at last the school grounds. I considered whether to try to walk with her and decided it would be the height of rudeness. Enough that in her blue skirt and white middy she would be half a block ahead and, from that distance, perhaps throw a glance in my direction, to bestow upon my heart a deserved and abundant blessing. I believed it was but right that in some such way as this her mission in my life was disguised.

Her name, I was to learn many years later, was a convenient mnemonic for the qualities to which argument might aspire. But in those days it was a living voice. "Oh that you might be worthy of uttering me," it said. And how

I endeavored to build my body so that I might live long to honor her. With every victory at singles at the handball court — the game was then the craze at school — I could feel my body glow in the sun as though it had instantly been cast in bronze. I guarded my mind and did not let my wits go astray. In class I would not allow a lesson to pass unmastered. Our English teacher could put no question before us that did not have a ready answer in my head. One day he read Robert Louis Stevenson's *The Sire de Maletroit's Door,* and we were so enthralled that our breaths trembled. I knew then that somewhere, sometime in the not too improbable future, a benign old man with a lantern in his hand would also detain me in a secret room and there daybreak would find me thrilled by the sudden certainty that I had won Aida's hand.

It was perhaps on my violin that her name wrought such tender spell. Maestro Antonino remarked the dexterity of my stubby fingers. Quickly I raced through Alard — until I had all but committed two thirds of the book to memory. My short brown arm learned at last to draw the bow with grace. Sometimes when practising my scales in the early evening, I wondered if the sea wind carrying the straggling notes across the pebbled river did not transform them into a Schubert's *Serenade*.

At last Mr. Custodio, who was in charge of our school orchestra, became aware of my progress. He moved me from second to first violin. During the Thanksgiving Day program he bade me render a number complete with pizzicati and harmonics.

"Another Vallejo! Our own Albert Spalding!" I heard from the front row.

Aida, I thought, would be in the audience. I looked quickly around but could not see her. As I retired to my place in the orchestra I heard Pete Saez, the trombone player, call my name.

"You must join *my* band," he said. "Look, we'll have many engagements soon. It'll be vacation time."

Pete pressed my arm. He had for some time now been asking me to join the Minviluz Orchestra, his private band. All I had been able to tell him was that I had my school work to mind. He was twenty-two. I was perhaps too young to be going around with him. He earned his school fees and supported his mother hiring out his band at least three or four times a month. He now said:

"Tomorrow we play at a Chinaman's funeral. Four to six in the afternoon. In the evening, Judge Roldan's silver wedding anniversary party. Sunday, the Municipal dance."

My head began to whirl. On the stage, in front of us, the Principal had begun a speech about America. Nothing he could say about the Pilgrim Fathers and the American custom of feasting on turkey seemed interesting. I thought of the money I would earn. For several days now I had but one wish, to buy a box of linen stationery. At night when the house was quiet I would fill the sheets with words that would tell Aida how much I adored her. One of these mornings, perhaps before school closed for the holidays, I would borrow her algebra book and there upon a good pageful of equations, there I would slip my message, tenderly pressing the leaves of the book. She would perhaps never write back. Neither by post nor by hand would a reply reach me. But no matter; it would be a silence full of voices.

That night I dreamed I had returned from a tour of the world's music centers; the newspapers of Manila had been generous with praise. I saw my picture on the cover of a magazine. A writer had described how many years ago I used to trudge the streets of Buenavista with my violin in a battered black cardboard case. In New York, he reported, a millionaire had offered me a Stradivarius violin, with a card which bore the inscription: "In admiration of a genius your own people must surely be proud of." I dreamed I spent a week-end at the millionaire's country house by the Hudson. A young girl in a blue skirt and white middy clapped her lily-white hands and, her voice trembling, cried "Bravo!"

What people now observed at home was the diligence with which I attended to my violin lessons. My aunt, who had come from the farm to join her children for the holidays, brought with her a maidservant, and to the poor girl was given the chore of taking the money to the baker's for rolls and *pan de sal*. I realized at once that it would be no longer becoming on my part to make these morning trips to the baker's. I could not thank my aunt enough.

I began to chafe on being given other errands. Suspecting my violin to be the excuse, my aunt remarked:

"What do you want to be a musician for? At parties, musicians always eat last."

Perhaps, I said to myself, she was thinking of a pack of dogs scrambling for scraps tossed over the fence by some careless kitchen maid. She was the sort you could depend on to say such vulgar things. For that reason, I thought, she ought not to be taken seriously at all.

But the remark hurt me. Although Grandmother had counseled me kindly to mind my work at school, I went again and again to Pete Saez's house for rehearsals.

She had demanded that I deposit with her my earnings; I had felt too weak to refuse. Secretly, I counted the money and decided not to ask for it until I had enough with which to buy a brooch. Why this time I wanted to give Aida a brooch, I didn't know. But I had set my heart on it. I searched the downtown shops. The Chinese clerks, seeing me so young, were annoyed when I inquired about prices.

At last the Christmas season began. I had not counted on Aida's leaving home, and remembering that her parents lived in Badajoz, my torment was almost unbearable. Not once had I tried to tell her of my love. My letters had remained unwritten, and the algebra book unborrowed. There was still the brooch to find, but I could not decide on the sort of brooch I really wanted. And the money, in any case, was in Grandmother's purse, which smelled of "Tiger Balm." I grew somewhat feverish as our class Christmas program drew near. Finally it came; it was a warm December afternoon. I decided to leave the room when our English teacher announced that members of the class might exchange gifts. I felt fortunate; Pete was at the door, beckoning to me. We walked out to the porch where, Pete said, he would tell me a secret.

It was about an *asalto* the next Sunday which the Buenavista Women's Club wished to give Don Esteban's daughters, Josefina and Alicia, who were arriving on the morning steamer from Manila. The spinsters were much loved by the ladies. Years ago, when they were younger, these ladies studied solfeggio with Josefina and the piano and harp with Alicia. As Pete told me all this, his lips ash-gray from practising all morning on his trombone, I saw in my mind the sisters in their silk dresses, shuffling off to church for the evening benediction. They were very devout, and the Buenavista ladies admired that. I had almost forgotten that they were twins and, despite their age, often dressed alike. In low-bosomed voile bodices and white summer hats, I remembered, the pair had attended Grandfather's funeral, at old Don Esteban's behest. I wondered how successful they had been in Manila during the past three years in the matter of finding suitable husbands.

"This party will be a complete surprise," Pete said, looking around the porch as if to swear me to secrecy. "They've hired our band."

I rejoined my classmates in the room, greeting everyone with a Merry Christmas jollier than that of the others. When I saw Aida in one corner unwrapping something two girls had given her, I found the boldness to greet her also.

"Merry Christmas," I said in English, as a hairbrush and a powder case emerged from the fancy wrapping. It seemed to me rather apt that such gifts went to her. Already several girls were gathered around Aida. Their eyes glowed with envy, it seemed to me, for those fair cheeks and the bobbed dark-brown hair which lineage had denied them.

I was too dumbstruck by my own meanness to hear what exactly Aida said in answer to my greeting. But I recovered shortly and asked:

"Will you be away during the vacation?"

"No, I'll be staying here," she said. When she added that her cousins were arriving and that a big party in their honor was being planned, I remarked:

"So you all know about it?" I felt I had to explain that the party was meant to be a surprise, an *asalto*.

And now it would be nothing of the kind, really. The women's club matrons would hustle about, disguising their scurrying around for cakes and candies as for some baptismal party or other. In the end, the Rivas sisters would out-do them. Boxes of meringues, bonbons, lady-fingers, and cinnamon buns that only the Swiss bakers in Manila could make, were perhaps coming on the boat with them. I imagined a table glimmering with long-stemmed punch glasses; enthroned in that array would be a huge brick-red bowl of gleaming china with golden flowers round the brim. The local matrons, however hard they tried, however sincere their efforts, were bound to fail in their aspiration to rise to the level of Don Esteban's daughters. Perhaps, I thought, Aida knew all

this.   And that I should share in a foreknow-
ledge of the matrons' hopes was a matter beyond love.   Aida and I could laugh together
with the gods.

At seven, on the appointed evening, our
small band gathered quietly at the gate of old
Don Esteban's house, and when the ladies arrived in their heavy shawls and trim *panuelos,*
twittering with excitement, we were command-
ed to play the "Poet and Peasant" overture.
As Pete directed the band, his eyes glowed with
pride for his having been part of the big event.
The multicolored lights that the old Spaniard's
gardeners had strung along the vine-covered
fence were switched on and the women remarked that Don Esteban's daughters might have
made some preparations after all.   Pete hid his
face from the glare.   If the women felt let
down, they did not show it.
The overture shuffled along to its climax
while five men in white shirts bore huge boxes
of food into the house.   I recognized one of the

bakers in spite of the uniform. A chorus of confused greetings, and the women trooped into the house; and before we had settled in the *sala* to play "A Basket of Roses" the heavy damask curtains at the far end of the room were drawn and a long table richly spread was revealed under the chandeliers. I remembered that in our haste to be on hand for the *asalto,* Pete and I had discouraged the members of the band from taking their suppers.

"You've done us a great honor!" Josefina, the more buxom of the twins, greeted the ladies.

"Oh, but you have not allowed us to take you by surprise!" the ladies demurred in a chorus.

There were sighs and further protestations amid a rustle of skirts and the glitter of earrings I saw Aida in a long, flowing white gown and wearing an arch of *sampaguita* flowers on her hair. At her command two servants brought out a gleaming harp from the music room. Only the slightest scraping could be heard because the servants were barefoot. As Aida directed them to place the instrument near the seats we occupied, my heart leaped to my throat. Soon she was lost among the guests, and we played "The Dance of the Glowworms." I kept my eyes closed and held for as long as I could her radiant figure before me.

Alicia played on the harp and then in answer to the deafening applause she offered an encore. Josefina sang afterward. Her voice, though a little husky, fetched enormous sighs. For her encore, she gave "The Last Rose of Summer"; and the song brought back snatches of the years gone by. Memories of solfeggio lessons eddied about us, as if there were rustling leaves scattering all over the hall. Don Esteban appeared. Earlier, he had greeted the crowd handsomely, twisting his mustache to hide a natural shyness before talkative women. He stayed long enough to listen to the harp again, whispering in his rapture: "Heavenly, heavenly...."

By midnight the merry-making lagged. We played while the party collected around the great table at the end of the *sala*. My mind travelled across the seas to the distant cities I had dreamed about. The sisters sailed among the ladies like two great white liners amid a fleet of tugboats in a bay. Someone had thoughtfully remembered — and at last Pete Saez signalled to us to put our instruments away. We walked in a single file across the hall, led by one of the barefoot servants.

Behind us a couple of hoarse sopranos sang "La Paloma" to the accompaniment of the harp, but I did not care to find out who they were. The sight of so much silver and china confused me. There was more food before us than I had ever imagined. I searched in my mind for the names of the dishes; and my ignorance appalled me. I wondered what had happened to the boxes of food that the Buenavista ladies had sent up earlier. In a silver bowl before me, I discovered, there was something that seemed like whole egg yolks that had been dipped into a bowl of honey and peppermint. The seven of us in the orchestra were all of one mind about the feast; and so, confident that I was with friends, I allowed my covetousness to have its way and not only stuffed my mouth with this and that confection but also wrapped up a quantity of those egg yolk things in several sheets of napkin paper. None of my companions had thought of doing the same, and it was with some pride that I slipped the packet under my shirt. There, I knew, it would not bulge.

"Have you eaten?"

I turned around. It was Aida. My bowtie seemed to tighten around my collar. I mumbled something, I did not know what.

"If you wait a little while till they've all gone, I'll wrap up a big package for you," she added.

I brought a handkerchief to my mouth. I might have wiped away bits of food there, if only I were certain there were such telltale signs. But there were none; and if I had said "No, thank you," I might have honored her solicitude adequately and even relieved myself of any embarrassments. I could not quite believe that she had seen me, and yet I was sure that she knew what I had done; and I felt all ardor for her gone from me entirely.

I walked away to the nearest door, praying that the damask curtains hide me in my shame. The door gave on to the veranda, where once my love had trod on sunbeams. Outside it was dark, and a faint wind was singing in the harbor.

With the napkin balled up in my hand, I flung out my arm to scatter the egg yolk things in the dark. I waited for the soft sound of their fall on the garden-shed roof. Instead I heard a spatter in the rising night-tide beyond the stone fence. Farther away glimmered the light from Grandmother's window, calling me home.

But the party broke up at one or thereabouts. We walked away with our instruments after the matrons were done with their interminable goodbys. Then, to the tune of "Joy to the World," we pulled the Progreso Street shopkeepers out of their beds. The Chinese merchants were especially generous. When Pete divided our collection under a street lamp there was already a little glow of daybreak.

He walked with me part of the way home. We stopped at the baker's when I told him that I wanted to buy with my own money some bread to eat on the way to Grandmother's house at the edge of the sea-wall. He laughed, thinking it strange that I should be hungry. We found ourselves alone at the counter; and we watched the bakery assistants at work until our own bodies grew warm from the oven across the door. It was not quite five, and the bread was not yet ready.

THE WIRELESS TOWER

M Y NAME *is Roberto Cruz.*
Honesty is the best policy.
I ought to have a better pair of shoes.
My favorite subject is history, but I like literature also.
What is a compound sentence?

Wondering what else to say, Roberto Cruz, the troop scribe, counted the number of lines he had used up: he had four more to write on before reaching the bottom of the page. He filled these with the names of his father and mother, and those of his brother and sister, and wrote in also their respective birth dates. Of the four birth dates, he had difficulty in remembering that of his father although it was his father's name he had written down first. Bert leaned on the wall boards and tried to refresh his memory. He stretched his legs and waited. A soothing comfort ran down his body, from the nape of his neck to his toes.

He watched the wind bending the grass on the side of the mountain directly before him. He felt he could taste the wind. There was a touch of bay leaf and, somehow, of cardamon, too, in the brush of the wind. He was reminded of Mother standing before the woodstove emptying the contents of a pot of *adobo* into the candy can which, later, the members of the troop, from Scoutmaster Ponte down, devoured to the last tidbit.

Then, like a lump in his throat, it came: the day and the month of his father's birth. He was not quite sure about the year. But I'm now fifteen, he reasoned out; Father married when he was twenty-five. Bert added the two numbers and finally worked his way toward a solution.

The wall at his back creaked. It was an old wall. The cottage, which was to have served as the home of the caretaker of the radio station, had never been lived in. At Bert's feet the boards were covered with sandlike droppings of woodworm that had lived up there in the ceiling. Bert pulled up his knapsack, which had lain at his feet, and now used it as a pillow. He pushed himself up and the wall creaked again.

The porch railings were down, like a strip of fence in an abandoned pasture. Nothing obscured Bert's view of the mountainside. It was a pleasant April afternoon, steeped in sunshine. There had been a plan, Bert had heard, to set up a radio station here. Somehow it had not come off. Bert wondered if rust, like the woodworm in the lumber, had heaped rich deposits at the foot of the tower. The structure seemed to hold on, though. There was already a legend that lightning had split the rod at the top. It must have been quite a storm. Bert decided he would go and find out.

He put his notebook flat on the floor and made a rough sketch of the tower. He rigged up the drawing with the crisscrossing steel strands which, in the real tower, rose a good hundred and twenty steps heavenward. As he counted, his eagerness grew.

He did not complete the sketch. Hurriedly, he jabbed a vertical line at the top of his steel structure. He marked it with an "X". At the bottom of the page he wrote out a reminder:

To Whom it May Concern:
I'll be up there.

He signed his name simply, *Bert Cruz*. He gave his address.

27 *Real Street*
Buenavista, Buenavista

Then, smiling to himself, he got up and looked for a small rock. He found one at the foot of the small heap which was what had been left of the three-runged steps of the cottage porch. He played with the rock, tossing it with his right hand and catching it with his left.

He walked back to where he had left his knapsack, counting the times he caught the rock in the cup of his left palm. It had held the stone at least five times. His notebook lay beside the knapsack. He picked it up and ran through the pages without looking at them.

Butterflies, birds, fishes, trees and flowers lived like immortals in those pages. Bert had an image in the back of his mind of the neat little sentences he had filled the other pages with. He tried to remember when it was that he had gotten into the habit of putting down things that way. He could not remember.

He placed the notebook on top of his knapsack and the small rock on top of the notebook, opened at the page where he had written his message. Then, now whistling, he walked down to the yard, over the rickety floor-boards of the porch, past the heaped-up ruins of the steps.

The nearest shaft of the tower was the south shaft and was twenty-five steps away. Four of those shafts squared off a base of perhaps a hundred square feet. Robust concrete blocks anchored each shaft to the mountain. The story was that there ought to have been two towers. People said the second tower was to have risen about five hundred feet farther to the north. There the hilltop leveled off less flatly than here on the south. Bert wondered not so much why this other tower did not rise out there but how the mountain would look with the two towers. He imagined the two towers making conversation under the stars. He thought of the words they might have said to each other, like two friends sitting in the dark, rocking their chairs gently, thinking they would live forever.

Almost, now, the other steel tower seemed real. Bert closed his eyes for a moment, afraid to see it there in the sunshine standing against the blue afternoon sky. Pressing his eyelids tight, he tried to throw off the vision. He did not want it at all. He did not care to get mixed up. He realized that in his notebook he had sketched only one tower.

The line of steps hung on the east side. The first rung was about nine feet off the ground. He had to jump a little to reach the bar. He let go, remembering that he had to roll up his sleeves. He folded the cuffs carefully and got his arms clear up to his biceps. Then he reached for the first bar again. He felt it smooth in his hand. He chinned his way up, wriggling his hips a little.

By swinging his legs forward and locking his feet fast behind the big shaft, he was able to let go of one hand and make a good try for the second bar. It was elaborate and, he believed, energy-consuming.

The steps were a foot apart. The vertical bars that held the rungs were a foot wide and ran parallel. Unlocking his feet apart, Bert let go and caught the swing of his body by slipping his whole arm through and quickly keeping himself upright on the ladder till his weight pinched tight a wee strip of the skin between his legs. He wished he had rolled up his trousers too but thought better of it now that the skin hurt a little.

He realized that he had still his shoes on. It was a canvas pair, black all round except for the soles, which were red. He raised his left foot and pulled the lace loose. He bent over, still safely arm-locked, and pushed the shoe off, tugging from the heel. In like manner, he shed off the other shoe.

This one bounced on hitting the grass but rolled off miraculously toward its mate. Bert thought this was a sign, an omen or something. He felt that if he had so wished, both shoes might have come together as in a show-window.

But the thought of omens disturbed him. He looked away and saw the holes in the roof of the cottage where the galvanized iron sheets had been wrenched loose by the wind. His eyes followed the rain-gutter where it cut an angle with the porch roof. Then his gaze dropped and he saw his knapsack and the notebook pale white, stuck under the weight of the rock.

Without being aware of it, Bert had gained ten more steps. He cleared an additional twenty without looking at the cottage again. Resting, he locked his arms on to the step that came level with his shoulder.

He did not realize how far up he had climbed until he saw beyond the trees on the south side of the mountain the road which led to the town. He followed the road as if he were going home. Suddenly he lost his way in the trees. When he found the road again, it was behind a dark grove of mangoes. The rustle of the leaves seemed to reach him, and somehow

this frightened him. It was of course the form
that the sound of the wind took, perhaps as it
blew past the shafts as if these were broken bits
of wire. At this thought, Bert got frightened.
He climbed yet higher, though. Something
seemed at stake. Feeling numb in the arches
of his bare feet, he slipped his leg over one step
to rest, as if he were mounted on a horse.

The road passed some bamboos and looked like a strip of tree-bark that bunched them
up. Then it turned to the beach and went past
the town cemetery. The grey walls appeared
like the line of barren paddy in a field. Because
the tombstones were not uniform, the field did
not resemble a strip of riceland. But it well
could have, judging from the length and turns
of the paddy. The wind was brisk now and it
seemed to bend the things that cropped off the
ground and which Bert identified as crosses.

He left his saddle now and diverted his
attention to the town slaughter-house which was
set on a rock that jutted out onto the blue harbor. There was an interisland ship at anchor,
the Nuestra Señora del Rosario. The super-

structure was unmistakable, hooded though it was with what looked like black canvas. Even the bridge had a forbidding shape. The hull was black too, and the men that crowded on the pier all looked as if they had only heads and no bodies whatsoever.

The road through the pier area rose black with mottled grey blots where moving objects, which Bert identified as carts drawn by carabaos, ranged in a shadow. The wide canopy of zinc, which was the Stevenson copra warehouse, might have glittered away like a great slab of silver. Actually, a cloud hung low over it, enshrouding the building with sheets of the dullest lead.

Bert looked up once. Huge masses of clouds, looking heavy like rocks, and as rugged at the edges, hung in a shelf over him. The wind chilled his back. It did not sing past the shafts now but began, it seemed, to tap the rivets loose. His feet confirmed their steadiness, though. Now the black ship at anchor in the harbor seemed to get smaller and smaller. The crowd at the wharf had begun to disperse and the dark spots scattered into the town until at last the streets seemed bare.

The wind turned. It blew straight at his face now, washing it clean. It was as if intent on cleaning even the dirt behind his ears. It scrubbed his hair and scalp. It rubbed his eyes and his cheeks and neck. He felt the sensation of bathing in dry water.

The more steps he cleared, the more intense the sensation became. Under his shirt the dry water of wind shrove him neatly. He once saw a movie in which there was a doctor scrubbing his hands and arms interminably. He felt exactly as if he were being cleaned up that way.

Then it came, a searing ache in the balls of his feet. It rose and seized his knees, gripping them as if with clamps. The wind grew still, suddenly. Sweat beaded on his back and across his waist, like a cross. His brow was dry, nothing bleared across his eyes, but he felt that tears would come any moment. He waited, making three steady steps, locking his arms each time.

He left like going down. For the first time, he did not feel equal to the landscape around. In his giddiness he imagined that the ground rose and sank. He could only look up at the clouds that lay in a shelf above him. An imaginary plumb line was being lowered for him. Suddenly the tip of the plumb line was fastened to the tower. It became the long vertical rod that he must reach. He canted his head, wondering why the rod seemed to move. He suspected it was an effect caused by some fault in his manner of looking.

He could not look long though to find out exactly what the trouble was. His sweat was heavier now, the pain in his bones had spread to his muscles. His calves knotted in tight bowlines and figures-of-eight. Even his neck was held in some awful knot; or rather, in that series of knots. He put his chin on one of the last steps, thinking that in that way he could rest. But his teeth began to chatter.

He held his jaw steady. Then after a brief rest his strength returned. He gained three more steps. He counted five more steps achieved that way. Then he began locking in three times in every case; this gave each foot a much longer spell of rest than before. He discovered that he could throw the entire weight of his body alternately on each foot. He felt the pull of the earth coming hard but the locks counteracted that, and suddenly he felt light.

There was nothing now between him and the rod but a narrow ledge. The steps ended here. But he did not want to get up the ledge. Somehow he had no desire to do it. He searched for the desire, as if he had brought it along like loose change in his pocket. Nothing jingled there. The weight of his sweat-beaded back and waist grew heavier again, and he could have slipped earthward from its drag alone. But he had his hands on the edge of the ledge now.

He knew from the tautness of his leg muscles that he had made it. He could feel the base of the steel rod now with the tips of his fingers. He closed his eyes for joy. He reached far out, farther out — for joy.

Thumb and forefinger circled the base of the rod. He wished they would meet, but the rod base was perhaps too large for that. The wind began to sing again. He could feel something like the strands of song at the tips of his thumb and forefinger. An entirely new sensation rose from the middle of his back and settled at the base of his skull. It was made of the wind's song, which came without sound, without a tune, even. And it seemed it would last forever.

He heaved over to get into position for another saddle-rest. His easy success was little short of a miracle, he felt. His hand gripped at the base of the rod still, and being able to reach farther now, finger- and thumb-tip met at the rugged edges which rose so many inches up on the skin of the rod. He could turn his grasp full circle. Whichever way he turned it, the rugged edges followed. He could feel the grit in his teeth and the tang of split metal on his lips. His nostrils flared. He caught the smell of rock, sun-bleached, born and bred of the sun's heat on steel. It seemed that the rod breathed.

And it was split. This was incontrovertible; he could speak about it without a doubt. His hands could be preaching it; it was gospel talk. He was dazed by the thought.

Something had been drained off his hands so that now it had no sensation left except the anticipation of the feel of the crack and the crevice and the length of the split. He reached again and again; he did not have to search. Each time, his joy came heady but his heart throbbed as if it would never stop.

Bert felt he could not stand it. This was too much to keep for so long. Slowly, and step by careful step, he retraced his ascent. The rock structure of clouds overhead had lifted and soft felt carpets of them seemed to have spread under the sun. He kept his gaze on the town. Now it glowed, roofs and streets and all.

Even the market place and the schoolhouse and the church, which he did not care to see before, emerged as if from shadows and called out to him. He saw the creek that ran past the market place and swept its bed dry to the lee of the harbor, and the pebbles glittered as if they were precious stones. The ship was still at anchor, but it had moved from its original position. Somehow a lid of water quivered between her hull, now an indifferent grey, and the cliff of the wharf. The red band on her funnel and three triangular flags that waved from the main mast caught Bert's delight. The flags seemed to wave to him. The ship offered her white-painted deck to his gaze and the bridge glowed with brass trimmings. Surely, she was on her way to another voyage. Smoke, white and lacy, emitted the message from the stack, and there was a new-looking crowd, well-wishers, gathering at the pier. Bert thought they were all umbrellas and hats, and as he cleared more steps on the climb downward, he recognized them as hands waving and waving.

The last few steps were easy. It was as if his muscles had not tightened up so rudely before. He leaped to the ground and sat on the grass and put on his shoes. Then he walked to the cottage, a little self-consciously — somehow afraid of himself.

He did not wish to hold up his head proudly, he had no desire to throw out his chest. He remembered the cemetery and the dark road through the trees he had seen earlier; and he did not care to swing his arms about.

He got to the tumbledown porch, picking his steps carefully, and sat beside the knapsack he had left behind. His notebook, with the pencil tied to it, lay as before under the small rock he had used as a weight. He put the rock away.

Once more he leaned on the old wall, and again it creaked. The sound was accompanied by a shower of woodworm droppings from the ceiling. Some fell on the notebook he held in his hand.

He laid the page open on his leg and wet his pencil tip again. Without reading what he had written, he set his pencil tip on a blank line.

Counting the next sentence he would write, he would have for the moment six of them altogether on the page: he would use the next line instead.

On this he wrote: *It is true.*